Windy

May he
always be
side.

James Baker

The Wooden Heart

A Contemporary Christian Romance

FRANCES BAKER

WESTBOW·
PRESS
A DIVISION OF THOMAS NELSON
& ZONDERVAN

WestBow Press books may be ordered through booksellers or by contacting:

WestBow Press
A Division of Thomas Nelson & Zondervan
1663 Liberty Drive
Bloomington, IN 47403
www.westbowpress.com
1 (866) 928-1240

ISBN: 978-1-4908-3104-6 (sc)
ISBN: 978-1-4908-3105-3 (hc)
ISBN: 978-1-4908-3103-9 (e)

Library of Congress Control Number: 2014905415

Printed in the United States of America.

WestBow Press rev. date: 03/17/2014

Dedication

To my mother, Thelma Walters, and
daughter, Danielle, for their
support and encouragement. To Dr. Edna Ellison
for her advice and to E. R. for inspiration.

CHAPTER

....

1

....

ome! Every turn of the wheels, every curve in the road brought Jennifer Kent that much closer to her beginnings—to all she had ever really known and loved. But the thrill and anticipation that had accompanied Jennifer on her previous treks to the isolated Northern California community of her childhood was no longer there—only the empty void of loneliness that had permeated everything around her since Ezra's death.

The majestic serenity of the coastal mountains and valleys no longer possessed the ability to uplift and inspire her soul. Now they only seemed to close in around her, encasing her in an inky-black cocoon of isolation, just as the skyscrapers of San Francisco had done.

Jennifer closed her eyes, her heart aching with a pain as fresh as the day her father had died just a few short months earlier. The sudden blast of a horn and a flash of blue and green heading straight toward her compact car quickly snapped her back to reality. Jennifer abruptly jerked her fast-moving vehicle back into its proper lane just in time to avoid a head-on collision.

Shaken by the near accident, Jennifer pulled her car to the shoulder of the road and rested her head against the steering wheel, allowing the tears of fear and frustration to run freely down her cheeks.

"Lady, just what do you think you're doing, trying to run me off the road?" came a deep, demanding voice from somewhere above her crouched position. Jennifer could only make out a large male form standing next to her car as she turned her tear-streaked face in the direction of the voice.

In an instant, the distant, harsh voice took on a quality of compassion and genuine concern as the stranger knelt beside the obviously distressed young lady who possessed the softest golden-brown hair he had ever seen. The beautiful waves of curls seemed to catch the rays of sunlight to form a soft aura of white gold around her head. He gently brushed a stray tendril of hair away from her dampened cheeks. There was both a delicacy and strength in her face that felt so exquisitely silky to his work-roughened hands.

"Are you all right? You're not hurt, are you?" he asked.

Jennifer didn't trust her voice to respond as she shook her head to let him know that physically, at least, she was fine.

"Just take a few deep breaths and calm down. No one was hurt, and no damage was done. Just try to relax. You should be fine in a couple of minutes."

The peaceful confidence evident in his voice seemed to say everything would be fine simply because he had wished it to be so.

Jennifer closed her eyes and rested her head against the back of the car seat. After a few seconds, she began to regain at least a semblance of composure. The soothing voice continued to comfort her with words lost in their salving balm as her heart began to once again return to its normal pace.

Feeling calmer, Jennifer opened her eyes and turned to reassure the stranger that she was indeed fine and truly sorry for the near-mishap. But the moment she turned toward him, she stopped. Her mind froze as she viewed her reflection in the deepest coal-black eyes imaginable—eyes that could never be the mirrors to one's soul, for they only reflected the image of the viewer. The intensity of their depth held her transfixed, as if she were being physically restrained.

The stranger's dark brows slanted into a frown. Jennifer failed to notice this change, but she did catch the beginning of a smile as it tipped the corners of his mouth, immediately softening his masculine features. A blush ran across her cheeks as she realized she had been openly staring at the handsome stranger.

"I'd say you're fine, miss. Just take it easy, okay?" The stranger straightened, and Jennifer watched his broad back as he casually traversed the short distance to his own vehicle.

She sat alongside the road for several minutes after the late-model blue-and-green truck disappeared around the bend of the highway, trying to rid herself of the feelings of foreboding and confusion that had overcome her in the space of their brief encounter. She was also surprised at the sudden chill she felt at the loss of his nearness.

Shaking off a slight shiver that ran up her spine, Jennifer started her car and was once again back on the road to her destination.

Despite her best intentions, she couldn't rid herself of the sensations that were plaguing her emotions. Throughout the rest of her drive, Jennifer felt the presence of the dark-eyed stranger watching her every move. Each time the speedometer crept higher than it should, she felt his frown of disapproval. Another shudder ran the full length of her slim body at the almost tangible nearness she felt toward this stranger—as if he were in some way her guardian angel. A brief smile touched her full lips at the thought.

It was almost sundown when Jennifer turned off Highway 101 onto Covelo Road. She began to feel herself relax. She was back in familiar territory. A couple of deer darted up the hillside. The Eel River, which flowed alongside the road, was a mere trickle of itself at this time of the year but could still prove to be a formidable enemy to those who were unaware of its treacherous secrets.

As she approached the last bend in the road, she felt her heart contract with both joy and apprehension. She pulled her car into the parking area of a scenic overlook and was pleased to find she had it all to herself. The heat of the warm summer day was abated slightly by a refreshing breeze being swept up the slopes of the hills surrounding the valley floor.

As she walked to the rail of the overlook, Jennifer felt her whole life was spread out before her in the thirty square miles that made up the remote valley. To her left lay the Indian reservation, such as it was. No one really knew the boundaries, and the houses looked just like the rest of the valley.

Jennifer smiled as she remembered the disappointed looks on tourists' faces when they first viewed the reservation. Nearly all were expecting a scene out of the great Southwest, not realizing that the transition to the "white man's world" had been fairly easy here.

The town—not much more than a cluster of old buildings and houses—lay almost directly in the middle of this gem of the California Coast Range. Most of the rest of the flatlands were broken up into small ranches and farms, none of them able to fully support any of the families that lived on them. To the right rose the steam and smoke of the giant Drake Lumber Mill, the major employer for most of the valley's residents.

Ezra Kent had spent almost twenty-five years of his life working at the lumber mill. Jennifer had never been able to understand why he had been so content to stay there when he could have moved on to a better-paying job somewhere else.

"A man can only be happy when he's where the Lord wants him to be and no place else," was always the answer her dad had given when Jennifer asked him why they didn't move.

Some people in this valley had never been more than twenty miles from home, never seen the skyscrapers of the city, never experienced so many things that were supposed to be important in making a happy life, yet they seemed content in their ignorance. They possessed a peace Jennifer had lost somewhere in her travels. Maybe in coming back ...

"I'm not so sure this is such a good idea," Jennifer said aloud to any creature that might be listening. What was here for her anyway but memories? And those same memories were causing her sleepless nights and loneliness.

With a sigh, Jennifer turned her back on the scene below and returned to her only real possession: her car.

"It's a little late now to be having second thoughts, young lady, so you might as well just go on."

Jennifer realized for the first time she was actually talking to herself out loud, and she shook her head as she slammed the car door shut. Rocks sprayed the parking lot as she reinforced her resolve with a burst of speed to complete the last couple of miles that separated her from the floor of the valley.

In the last five years, it seemed as if nothing had changed. The gas station still needed a new coat of paint. The kids still cruised the main street of town, stopping occasionally to visit with another group. The drive-in was open late for the summer crowd. The gift shop where you could find just about anything you might want was still in business, and it looked just as well stocked as always, from the appearance of the overcrowded front windows.

Jennifer turned off the main street and drove the two short blocks to the Kent home. She drove very slowly as the house came into view. The white picket fence needed to be repaired in several places. Jennifer remembered helping Ezra carry the boards and nails for the fence when she was only seven years old.

The giant black walnut tree in the front yard was still standing, but it too looked as if it would not be standing much longer. Jennifer smiled, thinking of all the sacks of walnuts she had picked up and sold every fall to earn extra spending money.

As she finally pulled into the driveway, Jennifer was surprised at how small the two-story house now seemed. When she was younger, it had seemed as big as a castle. It was her castle, and no harm could ever come to the enchanted people who lived there.

But that idea, like so many others, was just a fantasy. And fantasies have no place in the world of reality.

"Jennifer! It's about time you got here. I was beginning to worry." Mrs. Kent opened the screen door and walked down the steps to meet her daughter.

"One of these days, Mom, I'm going to get you a new apron," Jennifer teased, trying to hide the catch in her voice at the sight of her mother. She was the same slim, pretty lady she had always been, with the same white bib apron she had worn for as long as Jennifer could remember.

"What for? This is a new apron! I just happen to like the style."

Mrs. Kent embraced her daughter, and they stood silently for a few moments in each other's arms, deep in their own thoughts.

"It's good to be home," Jennifer said, breaking the silence as she moved away from her mother and began to gather her few pieces of luggage from the interior of the car.

"Child, these can't be all of your belongings?"

"No, Mom." Jennifer halted slightly, searching for just the right words to let her mother know her decision to come home was not final. "I still have three more months left on my lease yet, so I decided to leave most of my stuff in the apartment until I find a job."

"That's a good idea. I sure hope you find something here, but I haven't heard of anything yet. I'll do some calling around tomorrow and see if anyone knows who might be hiring. But let's worry about that tomorrow; we have tonight all to ourselves, just like we us't to when your father had to go out into the woods overnight. I've moved all my sewing stuff out of your old room so you can have it back."

Mrs. Kent picked up one of the smaller suitcases and headed up the back stairs.

Jennifer slowly reached down, picked up two more pieces of her luggage, and sighed. Nothing would ever again be like they once were now that her father would no longer be coming home. Jennifer felt a twinge of resentment creep into her heart at the almost-carefree attitude of her mother.

As she walked into the tiny kitchen, she could tell something was wrong. Something was missing. Jennifer couldn't put her finger on what it was, but something was definitely different. The faded yellow countertop was the same; so were the white appliances. The coat rack! The coat rack was gone! It had become almost a tradition as Jennifer was growing up that as soon as she heard her father's truck pull into the driveway, she would dash to the coat rack and hide behind one of the long coats that always hung there, winter or summer. Ezra had carved the hooks by hand and had always told her the wood in that rack would last as long as the old house stood.

Ezra would come through the door and demand, in a voice tinged with laughter, to know whether Mom had managed to get rid of that skinny kid who was always hanging around their house. Jennifer always managed to start giggling, and Ezra would make a big production of going through all the coats until he finally pulled away the one under which she was hiding.

Shaking his head, he would take her in his arms and announce that he guessed no one else would have her anyway, so they might as well just keep her.

Now it was gone!

"Mom!" Jennifer yelled in alarm as she stared at the vacant place on the wall next to the door.

"What is it, child?" answered Mrs. Kent as she entered the kitchen, a concerned frown on her face.

"It's gone, Mom. Where is it?"

"What's gone, dear?"

Jennifer pointed to the bare wall. "The coat rack! It's gone!"

"Oh, that. Well, I just decided to brighten up the place a little bit a few weeks ago and took it out to the garage, along with some other old pieces. I think I'll put up some little shelves and set some of my plants there. How do you think that would look?" Mrs. Kent spoke with a great deal of animation, not noting the distressed look on her daughter's face that her actions had caused.

"Mom, how could you?" Jennifer could no longer contain the frustration and anger she now felt. Running past her mother, Jennifer fled to the safety and security of her former room and fell sobbing across the four-poster bed that occupied a major portion of the small room.

The room was dark when she awoke from her troubled slumber. A soft knocking sounded against the door.

"Jennifer, are you all right?" Deep concern edged the softly spoken words. "May I come in, please?"

Jennifer sat up and rubbed her tired and burning eyes. Her head throbbed from the intensity of the emotions she was experiencing. Rising, she switched on the light next to the bed and walked across the room to the door.

"Come on in, Mom."

"Honey, do you feel like talking?" Mrs. Kent's pale blue eyes were darker than usual, reflecting her troubled state of mind.

"I guess," Jennifer replied in a soft voice as she returned to the bed and sat cross-legged in the middle of the dusty rose chenille bedspread.

"Jennifer, I think we need to talk," Mrs. Kent said, almost in a whisper.

"Mom, I'm not sure there's anything to be said."

"Don't you think I know what you're going through? I moved the coat rack because every time I looked at it, I saw your father coming home and playing that game with you, and it would hurt so bad I wanted to die just so I could be with him." Unshed tears glistened in the blue eyes that appealed for understanding. "But God has some reason for me to remain here on earth for a little longer, and I'm going to continue doing the best I can until it's time for me to go home, too. Honey, I wish I could help you through this time, but this is one journey you have to make by yourself, with God's help."

Jennifer bit back the words she wanted so desperately to say, but the grief she had already inflicted was more than she could stand.

"Mom, I miss him so much." The hoarse whisper caught in her throat as Jennifer hugged her pillow close to her stomach.

"I know, honey, I know." Mrs. Kent held her daughter close, as if she could take away some of the pain her child was experiencing.

"Let's both get some sleep and, maybe tomorrow will look a litter better. Besides, if you plan on doing any job hunting, you'd better get some beauty rest." Mrs. Kent gently cupped her daughter's face in her hands and smiled. "Not that you really need it."

It was easier to try to sleep than to hope to explain to her mother the depth of the feelings she was experiencing, so Jennifer merely shook her head in agreement.

"Good! I'll see you in the morning." Mrs. Kent spoke cheerfully as she kissed her daughter on the forehead, crossed the room, and closed the door behind her.

Jennifer looked around her former room. It was much the same as she had left it over five years earlier. The high school pennants and mementos were still able to bring a smile to her face. Those were such good times in her life. Maybe good times would come again. Maybe all she needed was some time to let her wounds heal. Maybe ... maybe was such an uncertain word.

Weariness seemed to be pressing her tired body back onto the soft comfort of the bed, and Jennifer allowed herself to succumb to its pressure. Tomorrow could hold so much or nothing at all; it was too overwhelming to think about tonight as she quickly drifted into the oblivion of sleep.

The smell of bacon frying and the warmth of the sun roused Jennifer from her dreamless slumber. She threw back the covers, slipped her feet into the shoes beside her bed, and then glanced at the wrinkled blouse and slacks she had slept in. Sighing deeply, she decided to go down for breakfast and change later.

"Morning, Mom," Jennifer called as cheerfully as she could manage this early in the day.

"Well, I was beginning to wonder if you were going to sleep all morning or not," Mrs. Kent teased as she removed the bacon from the skillet and piled it on a plate next to a stack of fresh pancakes.

As she stared at the generous amounts of food spread out on the table, Jennifer felt compelled to question her mother, "Are we having company for breakfast?"

"No!" Mrs. Kent laughed cheerfully. "I just thought you'd like a nutritious breakfast before you go out job hunting."

"I usually just have a cup of coffee in the morning."

"Oh, but you will have something to eat this morning, won't you?" The older woman surveyed the table thoughtfully.

A smile softened Jennifer's face at the loving kindness of her mother. "Sure, I'll have something, but don't expect me to eat like this all the time. I'd weigh a ton if I did."

The look of pleasure that brightened her mother's face was worth the few extra calories she was about to consume.

"I did some calling around this morning," Mrs. Kent offered as she scooped a large spoonful of scrambled eggs onto Jennifer's already overflowing plate. "And the only place that seems to be hiring right now is the mill."

"What could I do there?"

"Oh, it's not working for the mill exactly but rather for the security force they've hired recently. Think some of the other independent mills have been having a little trouble, and so they hired some security outfit as a group. You might want to check it out at least."

"Well, it is better than nothing. Didn't Andrea Elwell work there at one time?"

"Yes, but it's Andrea Combest now. She married the youngest Combest boy a year or so ago. You may not remember them; they may have moved here after you left."

Jennifer listened politely as her mother filled her in on all the recent happenings in the valley, adding a nod or yes here and there but not really hearing anything that was said, lost rather in her own thought for the future.

The hot summer temperatures sent ripples of heat across the asphalt as Jennifer drove down the nearly vacant county road to the parking lot of the Drake Lumber Mill. It was not yet 10:00 a.m., but the sun's intense glare promised to soar well over the hundred-degree mark.

After she pulled into one of the few spaces reserved for visitors in front of the main office building, Jennifer switched off the car's engine and opened her door, immediately feeling the full force of the swelter. Droplets of perspiration trickled down her neck under the thick mane of hair pulled back from her face and held securely with bright green combs that matched the color of her printed sundress. She brushed an imaginary wrinkle from the front of the dress and thought about how different this place was from the city. No one would have dreamed of going job hunting in such a casual outfit in San Francisco, but here in the valley, it was perfectly acceptable, and much more comfortable, Jennifer mused, as she climbed the few steps to the door of the modern glass and wood structure.

The refreshing blast of cold air was a welcomed relief as she entered the waiting area of the office.

"Well, I don't believe it! Jennifer! Jennifer Kent! What in the world are you doing here?" The pixie of a girl behind the desk smiled with delight as she rose and crossed the few short steps to the front counter.

"Andrea, how are you?" Jennifer asked brightly.

"Just fine now!" the younger girl teased playfully as she wiggled the fingers of her left hand in front of Jennifer's face.

"Congratulations. Mom told me. I'm very happy for you." Jennifer smiled at the obvious happiness her friend was enjoying.

"As pretty as you are, Jennifer, I would have counted on your being the first to find some lucky guy." Andrea's comment was half serious and half teasing.

"Maybe he's lucky he hasn't found me yet," Jennifer countered lightly.

"Seriously, what can I do for you?" Andrea asked, puzzled as to why her former best friend had come to her place of employment.

"Well, I'm looking for a job, and I heard you might be hiring."

"The only thing we have right now is a security position, but I'm not sure you'd want it, and the pay's not great."

"Any pay's better than none."

"You know, of course, that you wouldn't actually be working for the Drake Mill but rather for a security firm out of Eureka. But Mr. Drake still has the final okay on anything and anyone who works here." Andrea still seemed a little puzzled that Jennifer would even be considering the position. "Why don't you try getting a job as a secretary in some office?"

"Well, I might consider it except for two things. First, do you know of any openings anywhere in the valley?"

"Come to think of it, I don't know of any other jobs around. What's the second reason?"

"The second is I only type about twenty errors a minute," Jennifer answered very solemnly.

It took Andrea several seconds to catch the meaning of Jennifer's last statement before she burst into a flood of giggles.

"I'd forgotten about Mr. Walters's typing class. You always had to stay after class to try to finish an assignment."

"I did spend a lot of time trying to finish my assignments, but I spent more time just looking at Mr. Walters." Jennifer grinned as she remembered her first teenage crush on the handsome first-year teacher.

"I heard you had some type of office job in San Francisco."

"I did, but I was a bookkeeper; they never let me near a computer."

Just then the phone rang and Andrea had to return to her desk, but she quickly handed Jennifer a job application and pointed to a vacant desk before returning to her duties.

The tinted windows helped cut the glare of the summer sun and created a cool, relaxing atmosphere throughout the entire office area. The noises from the activities of the mill yard were unnoticeable unless someone opened an outside door. It was almost as if she were watching a big screen television with the sound turned down. Jennifer felt like a secret spectator watching the work going on about her.

Suddenly a flash of blue and green shook her from her trancelike state. A truck sped across the mill yard between the stacks of freshly cut lumber. It was the same truck she had almost hit. Jennifer froze in panic. That man couldn't possible work here. There was no way she could face him again after the way she had reacted to him.

"Andrea, who owns that blue and green truck that just went by?"

"Which one? There are about ten of those around here. They all belong to the company, but just about anybody could have been driving it. Mr. Drake is very generous with his equipment; he even lets people take them out of town occasionally if they need transportation. Why?"

"Oh, no special reason. It just looked familiar."

Maybe the man with the dark eyes had just borrowed the truck. At least she could hope.

Jennifer completed the application, handed it back to Andrea, and waited while Andrea answered yet another phone call. It really was too bad her secretarial skills were not better because this office really needed more help if today was typical of its activities.

"I'll give this to the company representative, and you should be hearing from him very soon. It's good seeing you again. Let's plan on having lunch one day soon, okay?"

Jennifer shook her head affirmative as Andrea reached to answer the still-insistent phone.

The day was still early, and Jennifer dreaded the thought of returning home as she headed her car toward the center of the valley floor and the small grouping of buildings that made up the town's business district.

Parallel parking had yet to arrive, Jennifer noted as she pulled her car into one of the diagonal parking spaces that lined the main street. Taking her time, she leisurely browsed from one shop to another, chatting with old acquaintances and marveling at the wide selection of items the shops had to offer for such a small area.

"Jennifer Kent!"

Jennifer didn't even need to turn around to know the identity of the person calling her name. "Reverend Hamilton. How are you?" Jennifer asked, not really caring what his answer might be.

"I'm just the same as always. Your mom said you were coming home. Is there any chance we might be hearing some special music from you one of these Sundays soon?"

The bright, cheery smile failed to thaw the chill Jennifer felt in the presence of this man of the cloth. "I don't know. I haven't done any singing since high school. But we'll see," Jennifer promised halfheartedly as she moved to the counter to make her small, unneeded purchase.

"We will see you in church on Sunday, won't we?" the pastor continued, undaunted.

"We'll see," Jennifer responded as she collected her change, picked up the parcel, and headed for the door.

She saw no other place to visit, and the mid-afternoon heat was taking its toll on her energy as Jennifer reluctantly turned her car down the street toward her parents' home.

"I'm glad you're home. I left some ice tea in the refrigerator. A gentleman called for you a couple of minutes ago. I left his number there by the phone," announced Mrs. Kent above the noise of her sewing machine.

"Thanks, Mom. Do you know who called?" Jennifer asked as she opened the refrigerator door for the iced tea and something to munch on.

"Don't recall his name, but he said it was about the job application you left at the mill this morning."

"That was fast," Jennifer replied more to herself than to her mother.

"What's that you said, dear? I couldn't hear you over my machine."

"I said I'll call him back now," Jennifer said, fabricating an answer for her mother's sake as she reached for the phone and began dialing the number on the bulletin board.

Several rings later, a graveled voice came across the phone.

"Drake Mill."

"This is Jennifer Kent, and I was given this number to call about a security position."

"You want one of the guards; just a minute and I'll get you one."

The loud noises of machinery roared in the background as Jennifer waited for what seemed an eternity. Finally the voice of an older gentleman resounded across the wires.

"Miss Kent, this is Lieutenant Edwards. I went over your application this afternoon, and if you could, I would like for you to come out here this evening for an interview and let me show you around the place a little bit."

"I guess that would be fine. What time should I come out?" Jennifer felt she really didn't need a tour because of all the times she had gone with her dad to check on some piece of equipment on a Saturday or Sunday. But from the looks of the buildings and grounds this afternoon, even the mill was not the place it had once been to her. The buildings were more modern, and everything seemed much more efficient than the way she had remembered.

"How about 7:00? Most of the crew should be gone by then, and it won't be quite so noisy."

"That sounds fine. See you then."

Jennifer couldn't help the feeling of dread that seemed to accompany the phone call. The man had said nothing ominous, but she had the uncomfortable feeling that something was about to happen, and she was not ready for another change in her life. The cloud of depression she had been under for months was beginning to lighten, but she wasn't ready for too many changes all at once yet. She needed a slower pace in her life. Wasn't that the main reason she had returned to this isolated valley?

CHAPTER

....

2

....

Carefully tucking her bountiful supply of rich golden-brown curls under the shell of her hard hat, Jennifer stood back to inspect the reflection the mirror before her. Despite the uncomplimentary headgear, the overall effect was pleasant. After her first day on the job at the mill, Jennifer had learned any attempt at makeup was fruitless. Between the dust of the mill and the heat of the Northern California summer sun, her complexion would either be streaked with perspiration or wiped completely bare within a matter of hours. She settled for a light moisturizer and a faint application of mascara to highlight the intensity of her bright blue eyes and quickly finished preparing for work.

She was still a little surprised at how well the interview had gone, and although she had not been particularly impressed with some of the other guards or with Lieutenant Edwards, she was actually looking forward to reporting to work.

Wincing at the stiffness she felt in her legs and trying carefully to avoid any of the numerous blisters on her toes and feet, Jennifer slowly made her way down the stairs of the Kent home and walked into the kitchen.

"It looks as if those blisters are beginning to get to you, dear," Mrs. Kent said sympathetically to her limping daughter.

"This too shall pass," Jennifer said theatrically as she filled her thermos bottle with the last of the coffee. "But I sure hope it's soon."

"I must admit, I really don't know how you can do it. I'd bet even the toughest men would find those blisters and sore muscles hard to take," her mother commented as she finished straightening up the kitchen.

"That's where the difference is: it takes a woman to be able to stand the pressure and pain of blisters." Jennifer grimaced. "I'll see you tomorrow," she called over her shoulder as she headed for the back door, pausing to study the concerned look on her mother's face. "Mom, please don't worry about me. I'm fine; other people are always there. Besides, all that walking is good for me."

"I know you'll be fine." Mrs. Kent moved closer to her daughter. "It's just that you and the Lord are all the family I have left."

Jennifer hugged her mother tightly for a few seconds and then broke the embrace with an excuse that she had to get to work.

Her mother's statement lay heavily on Jennifer's mind as she drove the few country miles to the mill yard. If she and the Lord were her mother's only family, then Jennifer had only her mother. It seemed so unfair to her to have only one other person in this whole world she could call her own. So unfair! So many aspects of life were unfair. Why had God taken her dad from her just when he could have retired and begun to take life a little easier? It just wasn't fair! Jennifer gripped the steering wheel a little tighter as she thought of the inequity that had changed her little world.

As she pulled her late model, medium-sized car into the employee parking lot spaces reserved for the security staff, her partner for the evening, Glen Hughes, was just collecting his equipment from his vehicle in the adjoining space.

Although they had worked only a couple of shifts together, Jennifer had the distinct feeling there would never be a time when she and Glen would share a good working relationship. For some reason, the man had taken an almost instantaneous disliking to her. Glen was easily in his mid-forties, with a stocky build. He was neither ambitious nor exceptionally intelligent. He did as little as possible with his assigned duties and could generally be found visiting somewhere in the mill with the regular employees. He made it quite evident to everyone that he was not pleased with the prospect of working with a woman.

"Heard you might want to check out the new schedule," Glen said with a hint of sarcasm as he passed Jennifer on the way to their temporary office area in the mill's lunchroom.

"Thanks," Jennifer replied as she watched the older man catch up with some of the mill workers heading to the lunchroom for their evening break.

The lunchroom was quiet as Jennifer walked to the schedule board. Graveyard shift! She had never in her life worked those hours. Sighing, she turned and came face to face with a very pleased Glen.

"At least you won't have to work with me," Jennifer offered with the sweetness of honey dripping from her lips. Not waiting for a reply from her coworker, Jennifer exited the confines of the small room.

Jennifer paused on the porch of the building and surveyed the scene, taking in the sights and excitement of the activities surrounding her, deciding this would be a good time to have one last look around the lumberyard in the daylight.

The Drake Lumber Company mill was the only one of its kind in Northern California and perhaps on the whole West Coast. In the few days she had been assigned to work there, Jennifer had ascertained from the regular employees that it was the most modern and efficient sawmill ever built. The complete sawing operation could be accomplished with only eight employees as opposed to the thirty men other mills required.

The sawmill building itself was a giant three-story steel structure housing workshops, all the saws, a few offices, and the computer center to run the entire operation. The rest of the yard area contained the huge decks of logs waiting to be cut, stacks of finished lumber, and several smaller buildings. An open one-story building set apart from the mill had been converted for use by the employees as a cafeteria, locker area, and meeting room. The main business office building was removed from the rest of the mill, insulated from the noise by large stacks of finished lumber.

The whole land area to be patrolled was close to eighty acres, about twenty city blocks. Each guard was expected to patrol some of the area for the better part of each eight-hour shift.

Several times during her aimless walk around the yard area, she caught glimpses of several of the blue and green mill trucks, but so far she had not noticed anyone who even faintly resembled the stranger she had met on the road.

"Jennifer!"

Catching sight of Andrea waving to her from the office door, Jennifer headed in that direction and hoped the cool office would offer some relief from the heat of the burning sun.

"I hoped I'd have a chance to talk to you soon," Andrea offered as she ushered Jennifer into the sanctity of the office. "What are you doing tomorrow for lunch?"

"I don't have any plans right now. Why?"

"I want you to meet my husband, David. He'll be off tomorrow, and we usually have lunch in town. We would like you to join us."

"I don't know. Maybe you two would like to have some time alone?" Jennifer hedged, reluctant to intrude on the twosome.

"Nonsense! If we didn't want you to join us, we wouldn't have asked." Andrea refused to take no for an answer and was not going to let Jennifer out of the engagement.

"Okay. I'd better take you up on it; seems like it may be my last chance for a while." Jennifer offered a playful grin.

"You're not leaving again, are you?" Andrea asked, surprised and disturbed at the thought.

"No!" Jennifer teased. "Worse than that, I've been transferred to the graveyard shift."

"Oh no! I don't know which is worse." Andrea wrinkled her nose in disgust.

"Well, at least it will be nice and quiet. And I'd better get back to work while I still have a job. See you tomorrow at the restaurant about twelve?"

"Sounds perfect," Andrea called after her as the door closed behind Jennifer's back.

The rest of the shift went smoothly, and Jennifer found her thoughts drifting often to Andrea and her husband and the happiness so evident on the face of her longtime friend. She really didn't want to intrude on her friend's time with her husband but could think of no way out of the engagement without hurting Andrea's feelings. Finally she decided that, if nothing else, she would claim she wasn't hungry and ask to be excused as soon as the introductions were over.

The traffic on the main street had picked up for the lunch crowd as Jennifer stepped onto the sidewalk that ran along part of the business district. The eatery was nothing compared to those found in a bigger city, but for this small town it wasn't bad. Besides, it was the *only* restaurant in town.

The ceiling fans turned silently above the hum of the diners as Jennifer walked into the large open room.

"Jennifer! We're over here!" Andrea called from a group of tables along the wall of the room. The waiters had moved several tables together, and Jennifer saw only a sea of green and tan surrounding the long tables.

Jennifer headed in that direction, and immediately the green-and-tan sea opened to provide a space in the midst of the nearly all-male gathering.

"This is my friend, Jennifer Kent," Andrea announced as soon as Jennifer sat down at the table next to her. "And this, Jennifer, is the California Department of Fire summer crew—or at least most of them."

Jennifer nodded to the group and looked to Andrea for some sort of explanation.

"David is a fire captain at CDF, and his unit just got back into the valley yesterday from fire detail, so this is kind of a celebration," Andrea whispered with a conspiratorial smile.

Several of the young men introduced themselves to Jennifer, while others of the crew offered their own words of advice as to who among their group could or could not be trusted with a pretty young lady. The hour passed quickly as Jennifer enjoyed being the center of attention, second only to the food they were served for lunch.

"Oh no! I'd better hurry and get back to work or Mr. Drake will have my hide," Andrea exclaimed as she glanced at her watch.

"I thought you said he was fairly easy to get along with?" David questioned his wife as she collected her purse and keys.

"He usually is, but lately something has really been bothering him, and is he a bear! See you at home, honey. Jennifer, you'd better get some rest if you're going to start that new shift tonight," Andrea said as she scooted off the seat and planted a light kiss on her husband's lips.

"I think you're right," Jennifer agreed as she, too, began to collect her purse and search for her car keys, silently thankful that her friend had given her the opportunity to make a graceful exit.

Several of the firefighters expressed their displeasure at her departure and asked if she would be around town for a while. After assuring them she was not going to be leaving soon, they finally allowed her to leave, and she headed home to try to get some rest before starting her new assignment.

The night skies were filled with the bright, glittering of stars, the moon shone with the brilliance of noonday, and the peacefulness of the country night was broken only by the occasional flurry of wings in flight or the crickets along the road. The sight of the mill complex always managed to give Jennifer a feeling of awe whenever it came into view, but the exquisite night scene that spread itself before her as she drove down the road was especially impressive. The large outdoor lighting system, easily seen for miles, was the first sight travelers picked out whenever they topped the ridges of the surrounding hills and gazed upon the valley stretching out below them.

Everything was quiet as Jennifer entered the office area. No one was in sight, and the guards' equipment was gone. Jennifer knew her coworker for the evening had already begun the mandatory rounds of the different checkpoints of the mill. Realizing this would be a good time to check out the log decks and perimeter, Jennifer left a message notifying her partner of her destination and then set out on her trek.

Always before, the task had been an easy one because she had completed it during the daylight hours. However, with only the aid of a flashlight, it was proving to be quite an undertaking. The ground was uneven and rocky. If she watched where she was walking, it did no good to patrol the area since she was unable to see either the fence line or the log decks. On the other hand, if she used her meager light to check the surrounding area, she couldn't see where she was walking. As a result, Jennifer found herself walking a few steps, stopping, checking the logs or fence line, walking a few more steps, and repeating the painstaking, slow process.

On more than one occasion, several of the mill workers had already warned her about the chances of spotting a rattlesnake making its home among the logs and sometimes coming out at night to take advantage of the sun-warmed soil. Jennifer listened carefully for any noise that might give her warning that one of the foreboding creatures was close at hand.

She had also been cautioned about the occasional slippage of logs from their storage decks. Although this was more likely to occur on the watered-down decks, the danger was still present on any of the massive stacks of logs. If the logs fell and someone happened to be in the way, it could be hours—maybe not until sunrise—before anyone would be able to locate them.

A rabbit scurried across her path and startled her out of her deep concentration.

"I've got to find a better way to do this," Jennifer called to the fleeing bunny.

Jennifer shook her head at the inefficiency of the task and the danger too. Suddenly an idea began to form in her ever-active brain. She found the perfect solution to her present dilemma: tomorrow night when she reported to work, she would bring her dad's old Jeep. No one had used it much since his death, but if she remembered correctly, it was still in good working order. The headlights could provide extra lighting. The vehicle itself could provide greater mobility, plus protection from snakes and sprained ankles. Besides, she could patrol more of the territory with less effort and far more efficiency. The vehicle was open, so no question would arise about it being used to conceal any stolen property from the mill.

"That, my dear, is a great idea!" Jennifer said aloud and smiled at the ingenuity of her solution.

The rest of the shift was uneventful. Jennifer found herself in high spirits for the first time in a very long time and was eager for a chance to try out her new plan.

Jennifer spent most of her waking hours the next day checking the Jeep to ensure she would have no mechanical difficulties and then making the vehicle as presentable as possible. Even Mrs. Kent was enthusiastic about the project and helped her daughter as much as she could.

The sight of Glen's car in the parking lot as she drove the Jeep onto the mill yard didn't dampen Jennifer's enthusiasm in the least. After explaining her idea to the rest of the crew, Jennifer was pleased to find everyone as excited about the prospect of making their job a little easier as she had been. Only Glen failed to express any opinion on the subject and went about his usual business, ignoring the other security personnel.

"He probably doesn't think it's a good idea because a woman thought of it," Jennifer muttered to herself as she climbed aboard the Jeep to begin her first patrol.

The shift passed incredibly fast. The vehicle worked out even better than anyone had imagined. Glen refused to drive it during his turn to patrol the yard, but Jennifer was thankful since he probably would have managed to get it stuck somewhere and then caused a fuss about the whole idea.

When she neared the end of the shift, Jennifer was surprised to find Glen going out of his way to be nice to her.

"Hey, Jen, why don't you take the equipment to the office this morning?" he said, puzzling Jennifer by his actions.

"I thought you liked to have coffee with the others in the mornings," Jennifer said, questioning his sudden change of heart.

"It's nothing special, and I thought maybe you'd like to show off the Jeep."

Jennifer gathered the equipment and placed it carefully in the passenger's side of the vehicle. Still wondering about Glen's sudden change of attitude, she began the short drive to the opposite side of the yard. Whatever his reason might be, she decided it made no difference to her. He had been right about one thing: she was delighted at the prospect of showing off her resourcefulness to those in command. The smirk of satisfaction crossing Glen's face as she drove down the dusty driveway went unnoticed by any of his coworkers.

Several of the regular employees waved and called good morning to Jennifer as she passed by. The bright sun shining in the cloudless sky promised a typical California summer day ahead.

CHAPTER

....

3

....

J arrod Drake impatiently stirred the thick black coffee in his cup. These past few days had been rough on him. How many months ago had he petitioned to God in his prayers for someone to share his life with? Until now, he had just taken it for granted that God would bring that special person into his life. But he was now well over thirty, and prospects were beginning to look pretty slim. An amused smile touched the corners of his mouth. The situation was so bad, in fact, that all he could think about was that brief encounter of a few days ago on Highway 101. That beautiful head of hair the color of a newborn fawn sunning itself in the warmth of spring's first golden rays, eyes as blue as the clear coastal skies ... he could still remember the velvet softness of her cheek as he had tucked a stray lock of hair behind her ear. He hadn't even made an attempt to find out her name or even where she was headed.

Jarrod mentally scolded himself for his flights of fantasy. He had enough problems here at home without adding an overactive imagination to them. Already this morning at least ten of the workers had stopped to ask about the Jeep the security guards had apparently driven around the yard area all night. He could just see some of those guards racing around the log decks and managing to get seriously injured. This was one problem he was going to eliminate immediately.

"Hey, boss, here comes one of the guards in that Jeep now!"

Jarrod gulped down the last of his coffee as he waited the arrival of the unsuspecting guard who would be the unfortunate recipient of his reprimand.

When she arrived at the impressive wood-and-glass office building, Jennifer gathered her gear together and marched toward the structure with a smile on her face.

When she opened the door, she was stunned by the deep commanding voice almost yelling at her.

"That is a private vehicle, and at *no* time are *any* private vehicles allowed on this property. Who gave you permission to bring it on the yard?"

Turning in the direction of the voice, Jennifer came face to face with the same dark eyes she had confronted on the highway. The smile slowly slipped off her face as she was once again held in the grip of those mesmerizing eyes. Everything else around her was reduced to a blur as she fought to break away from the power those dark eyes were holding over her.

Jennifer dared not hope that this stranger would not remember their earlier encounter, and the thought added to her already sinking despair.

"I want that vehicle off the yard. *Now!* I never want to see it here again. Do you understand?" The man continued speaking to Jennifer, oblivious to the other workers present in the room.

Slowly the rest of the room began taking shape around the stunned girl. Several of the department heads were gathered about the room drinking steaming cups of coffee, and all other conversations had ceased as they watched the two with intense interest. The gentleman who had spoken to her with so much authority was sitting on the bench alongside the wall with several others, his long legs stretched with ease across the pathway, blocking entrance to the rest of the room.

His plaid flannel shirt and worn blue jeans were molded to his large and powerful frame. Other than the pure force of his formidable stature and deep, commanding voice, nothing set him apart from the other mill workers in the room, most of whom appeared to be in their thirties or forties.

Irritation began to creep up her spine at the belittling way this man was treating her in front of a room full of strangers. Pulling her shoulders back and tilting her chin higher than was necessary, Jennifer turned to face the demanding stranger.

"Just who do you think you are anyway, ordering me around as if you owned the place? You're certainly not Mr. Drake, I know that for sure," Jennifer retorted, her courage growing bolder with each word.

"What makes you say that?" The gentleman's hostile disposition was beginning to give way to traces of humor.

Those same dark eyes that only moments ago had belittled and condemned her with their gaze were now holding her to ridicule, almost as if they knew some private secret.

"Because my father once worked for Mr. Drake, and he should be in his late sixties by now. You are not anywhere near that age! As for that vehicle, I'll have you know it saved us a lot of time last night and made the whole security force a lot more effective. I'm sure Mr. Drake would be pleased to know we're making good use of our time and his money. Now if you'll excuse me, I have more important things to do with my time than to stand around here and watch you sit and drink your coffee all morning."

Her stance radiated confidence as she placed the security equipment on the secretary's desk and walk toward the door.

"I don't believe we've been properly introduced. You must be Jennifer Kent. I'd heard the security company had hired you to work for them. I must say, you have a good memory, Miss Kent." The self-assured speaker rose from his seat and walked across Jennifer's path to the coffee urn on the opposite side of the room, blocking her well-planned retreat.

His casual stance belied his true height of well over six feet. His shirt strained across the broad expanse of his chest as he took a deep breath before continuing his conversation.

"I'm Jarrod Drake, and you're right, my father would have been sixty-eight on his next birthday." The dark-eyed man's voice had taken on a softer, slower tone as he watched the changes taking place of Jennifer's surprised face.

"Your father?" Jennifer questioned, not quite sure she had heard what was said.

A broad grin warmed the stern face as he waited for Jennifer's next course of action.

"I'm sorry, Mr. Drake, but I didn't know," Jennifer said, stumbling with her apology.

"Do you always display so much emotion, Miss Kent?" His innocent question hid a wealth of meaning when paired with the sparkle that radiated from the depths of Jarrod's dark eyes.

Jennifer groaned. *He remembered!*

"Now that we understand each other, I'd appreciate it if you'd please remove your vehicle from *my* mill yard." Jarrod held her in his gaze for a brief moment and then returned to the bench along the wall of the room.

Turing on her heels, Jennifer sought the safety of the outdoors to escape from the confines of the small office area, made even more suffocating by the presence of Jarrod Drake.

Jennifer felt resentment and anger building inside her as she reached to open the door to her freedom. At that same moment, Glen was making his usual appearance at the morning coffee session. The two security guards collided into each other, much to the amusement of everyone present. Jennifer was knocked backward by the sudden impact and fell soundly against the broad chest of one of the workers. Strong, masculine arms encircled her waist, preventing her from falling seat first onto the hard wooden floors of the building. The full body of her lush, shoulder-length curls she had worked so hard to hide under her hardhat tumbled in riotous disarray about her face as the hat clattered to the floor.

Jennifer was embarrassed as she turned to thank the worker who had caught her during her flight backward and was surprised to find herself looking into the smiling face of Jarrod Drake.

"Do you make it a habit of running into people, Miss Kent, or is it just me?" Amusement played on the features of his face so close to her own.

"Excuse me, Mr. Drake," she offered with a touch of frost on her words. Bending to retrieve her hat, she hoped to make a safe exit without further incident.

"Don't forget about getting that Jeep off the yard," he admonished her gently.

"Didn't she have permission from you, Mr. Drake?" Glen asked, trying to make his statement appear innocent, all the time refusing to look at Jennifer. "If I'd known, Mr. Drake, I sure wouldn't have allowed her to bring it on the yard."

"That little weasel!" Jennifer muttered to herself as she walked back to her parked vehicle, refusing to listen to anymore of Glen's insinuations.

"How dare they treat me like a child and not even give me a chance to explain!" Jennifer shouted to the wind as she gripped the steering wheel and sped through the gate and into the parking lot. "I'll show them a thing or two."

Jarrod found it hard to suppress the smile that softened his stern features as the sound of flying gravel and spinning tires penetrated the normal noises of the mill.

Standing, Jarrod stretched the full length of his solid frame before speaking, "Guess it's time to get this day underway," he said, thus signaling the end of the coffee session and time to get to work.

Traversing the small entry space of the room, Jarrod entered his own comfortable office and closed the door.

"Thank you, Lord." Joy filled his heart as he watched the activities on the mill yard. God had answered his prayers, he had no doubt.

Jarrod chuckled as pictures of a skinny little kid with dirty blonde pigtails came to his mind. Jennifer Kent had not been an outstanding beauty as a child, but that had sure changed. She still possessed that stubborn streak that had more than once gotten her into a scrape or two. In a way they were a lot alike, with many of the traits that being an only child seems to manifest.

Ezra had always been more than willing to relate the latest of Jennifer's escapades up until the time she had left for San Francisco. He never spoke much about her after that and had seemed burdened and sad about the situation for some reason. Most people just blamed the change on him missing his only daughter, but Jarrod had always suspected something deeper was at the heart of it.

A frown crossed his brow as he remembered the last time he had encountered Jennifer that afternoon alongside the highway. He saw again the pain and despair reflected in her dark, beautiful eyes. For all her stubbornness and determination, something was troubling her.

The buzz of the intercom broke into Jarrod's thoughts as he took a deep breath and resolved to pray daily for the beautiful woman God had brought into his life.

Anger still seethed in her heart as Jennifer drove the Jeep into the tiny one-car garage of her mother's home.

"Mother!" Jennifer shouted as she slammed the backdoor behind her.

"What is it, dear?" Mrs. Kent called from the living room.

"Why didn't you tell me?" Jennifer asked, continuing her display of anger as she marched into the adjoining room.

"Now calm down, dear. Tell you what?"

"About Mr. Drake."

"Dear," Mrs. Kent laid aside her knitting, "I did tell you that Mr. Drake passed away about two months after Ezra. Maybe you just don't remember."

"Well, when did Jarrod take over the mill?" Jennifer continued, reason taking over for her anger.

"Oh, Jarrod's been running the mill for about four years now. He's the one who made all the new changes. Ezra really admired the way that young man's improved conditions around there, making the whole process so much more efficient. Old Mr. Drake was content to continue with the way they had always been, but not Jarrod. He's such a nice young man too."

"Well, that's a matter of opinion."

During the next couple of days, Jennifer avoided any personal contact with Jarrod Drake. Instead, she used the guards' daily reports to bombard him with safety violations and ideas to improve the efficiency of the mill and the security service, including numerous reasons why a vehicle would be beneficial to their duties.

Early one morning about a week after her confrontation with Jarrod, Jennifer found herself in the tiny mill lunchroom with several of the mill's regular employees. As she bent to get a cup of coffee from the dispensing machine, Glen's voice rose above the general murmurs of the room.

"I don't see why anyone would put a woman on a security post late at night. Besides watching the mill, I've got to make sure the little girl there doesn't get herself into trouble too."

Jennifer slowly straightened and looked Glen straight in the eye. "I wouldn't worry about me if I were you, Glen. I can take care of myself."

"Now listen to the brave little girl talk! She couldn't even get out of the main office the other day without falling on her rear and right into Mr. Drake's arms. Or maybe that's what she'd planned to do and ensure herself of a nice, easy job around here," Glen stated with a smirk. "What if one of these guys came up and grabbed you from behind? Do you still think you could take care of yourself, or would you just fall into their arms too?"

"Glen, I'm not going to argue with you. I know I can take care of myself," Jennifer replied with calmness she wasn't sure she felt as she glanced around the all-male audience.

"Just how do you plan to do that?" Glen asked with a snort.

"Why don't you try it?" Jennifer offered along with an extra-sweet smile.

Suddenly all other conversations ceased, and Jennifer and Glen became the center of attention.

"Go ahead, Glen!"

"Put the lady in her place!"

"Yeah, the kitchen!"

Goaded by his comrades and an overinflated self-confidence, Glen rose from his seat at the table and began to walk toward an open space between the tables the mill workers had provided for this little exhibition of male superiority, with no doubt of the outcome in their minds. Glen outweighed the girl by at least fifty pounds. Several of Glen's friends placed small wagers, with but a few backing the bold young woman in their midst.

Everyone was much too involved with the spectacle to notice the tall, dark form standing near the doorway of the building, watching the scene with thinly veiled amusement twinkling in his eyes.

Word of the event spread like a wildfire, and just as Glen reached the area behind Jennifer, a small group of workers, eager to get a better view of the proceedings, shoved their way through the doorway, propelling the onlooker standing there toward Jennifer's back. Glen stepped quickly out of the way of the oncoming object. Jennifer, thinking it was Glen, grabbed the arm of the person behind her as he briefly came into contact with her shoulder and executed an expert judo throw. The unexpected weight and height of her subject caused Jennifer to lose her balance as she found herself also tumbling to the floor, landing with a thud atop her unsuspecting victim.

A quiet hush fell on the room as a tangled maze of limbs came to rest on the cold, hard floor of the lunchroom before them, a very surprised Jarrod Drake and an equally surprised Officer Kent sprawled atop him. Only the work whistle broke the silence. All the mill workers rushed to punch their time cards and exit the room, unwilling to be witnesses to the angry scene they knew was about to take place.

All the air had been knocked from Jennifer's lungs by her sudden collision with the rock-hard body now lying beneath her. As she took a deep breath of fresh air, all her senses were assaulted with the rich, clean scent of soap and fresh smell of new-cut wood that clung to his clothes and person. For the space of a moment, Jennifer was only aware of the distinctive face inches from her own. She could see only the dark eyes that were shining with unspoken laughter and a pair of lips so close to her own that were more exciting than any she had ever dared to dream existed. The only sound she was aware of was the rapid beating of her own heart.

Jarrod quickly stirred Jennifer from her trance-like state as he firmly set her on the floor and rose to his feet, pulling her along with him. He began to dust himself off, saying nothing to either Jennifer or the few remaining workers still trying to leave.

As the seriousness of the situation began to sink in, Jennifer sank dejected onto one of the lunchroom chairs. Her moment of triumph had once again turned into a moment of horror. For once she was sorry for ever having taken those self-defense classes while she lived in the city.

After what seemed an eternity to Jennifer, Jarrod spoke with a great degree of calm and tenderness.

"I do hope you don't plan to continue meeting me this way, Miss Kent. There are much easier ways to become acquainted. But I must admit, this does have some interesting possibilities." His face shone with all the mischievousness of a little boy plotting a playful prank on a buddy.

"Why does it seem I'm always saying *I'm sorry* to you?" Jennifer replied.

A soft chuckle escaped Jarrod's lips. "I must admit I've been looking for you, Miss Kent, but I hadn't planned on bumping into you, so to speak, in quite this manner." Sitting down in the chair opposite hers, he said, "I wanted to check and see how your hand is doing."

"My hand?" Jennifer asked, taken back by his calm manner.

"Your hand, Miss Kent! I just figured you must be suffering from writer's cramp with all the reports I've been getting from you. Yes, I've read every one of them." A pleasant grin crossed his face as he continued. "I just thought you'd like to know I agree with your suggestions about the Jeep, but I can't do anything about it because of our insurance restrictions."

"But what about the mill workers with trucks on the mill yard?" questioned Jennifer, puzzled by the whole situation.

"They are performing various functions for the mill, whereas, technically, you don't work for the mill, Miss Kent, but rather for the security company. If they see fit to provide a vehicle and insure it, then I have no objection. But until that time, you and all the other guards will continue to *walk* the yard. Do I make myself clear?"

When he finished his statement, Jarrod watched Jennifer's reaction. He could see her struggle to hold her tongue and not argue with him. Here was a woman who refused to be submissive or a follower. Nodding, he rose from his chair and walked out of the building, not giving Jennifer a chance to say anything she might regret.

Jarrod Drake had spoken, and as far as he or any of his employees were concerned, his word was law, not to be questioned but to be followed. No amount of pressure or persuasion in any form would make any difference in the outcome of the situation. Jennifer could feel only anger and bitterness as she sat alone in the empty building.

She could at least be thankful she hadn't been fired on the spot, but still, the knowledge that once Jarrod made up his mind no one could change it did little to lift her sagging spirits. The realization of her own responses to his presence disturbed her more than even the idea of losing her job. The less she saw of that man in the future, the better she would like it.

That evening the doorbell rang just as Jennifer and her mother were finishing the last of the dinner dishes.

"I'll get it." Mrs. Kent left the kitchen for her daughter to finish cleaning up.

The door opened, and the voice of Lieutenant Edwards drifted into the kitchen. Quickly drying her hands on the dish towel next to the sink, Jennifer joined her mother in the living room.

"Good evening, Miss Kent. I've heard so many nice reports about you. It's a pleasure to see you again. I do hope you don't mind this unannounced visit, but I was on my way to the mill for a little surprise inspection and wanted to come by and offer you my personal congratulations on your promotion and to give you your new stripes." Lieutenant Edwards handed Jennifer a small plastic bag containing several new arm patches and military-type stripes.

"What promotion?" A note of surprise penetrated the otherwise calm exterior Jennifer was trying to evoke.

"Didn't anyone give you my message? Didn't Mr. Drake tell you?"

"I'm sorry, Lieutenant Edwards, but I don't know what you're talking about."

"You've been selected to be the site supervisor of the security force at the Drake Lumber Mill. This position holds the rank of sergeant. A nice raise come with it too." Edwards smiled as he relayed this last tidbit of information, as if it were the *piece-de-resistance.*

"Just what does this involve, and why me?" Jennifer questioned as she perched on the edge of the early American sofa in the Kent's small living room.

"All I know is I got a call from our district office this morning, and they told me you had been selected from all the guards at the mill to be in charge out there. Your main responsibility will be to keep Mr. Drake happy with our services and to report to him on a daily basis—except on your days off, of course. You'll be in charge of scheduling shifts, hiring, firing, and making sure all the shifts are covered."

Lieutenant Edwards, noting her hesitation, continued, "You won't have any problem in taking the position, will you, Miss Kent?"

"Oh no! I'm just a little surprised, that's all."

"Well, I'm sure you'll do an excellent job. Besides, if you have any problems, just feel free to give me a call and I'll be more than happy to come and help you out. You are to report any unusual happenings to me, and I'll be calling at least once a week for your time sheets and checking on your supplies and the like. I'm sure we'll have a very good working relationship, so don't you worry your pretty little head about anything."

The smile and pat on the shoulder were meant to infer far more than he was saying, but Jennifer chose to ignore his true meaning.

"Well, I've imposed on you two charming ladies much too long, and I do have several other stops to make, so may I again offer my congratulations, and as I said, please feel free to call me at any time." With that, Lieutenant Edwards bade the two women goodnight and departed.

"Oh, Jennifer, this is really exciting. I'm so proud of you!" Observing the concerned look on her daughter's face, Mrs. Kent continued, "What's the matter, dear? You don't seem pleased. I know you can do the job. So what's troubling you, child?"

"Jarrod Drake!"

CHAPTER
4

The next few days were not as unpleasant as Jennifer had anticipated. Although she reported to Jarrod's office daily for supplies and to turn in reports, she seldom encountered him.

Round Valley, like most small communities, had only one major industry, and that was the Drake Lumber Mill. Many of young people who went to school with Jennifer went straight to work at the mill after graduation, just as their fathers had done before them. It was easy to renew old acquaintances among the many employees, so she was not surprised one morning when David Jefferies stopped to visit just as she was leaving the main office building.

"Jennifer, if you're not busy Friday night, how about going to the show with me? I promise I'll have you back before the stroke of midnight." An easy grin broke across David's boyish face.

They had dated once in a while during their high school days and always seemed to enjoy each other's company without any strings attached. The thought of spending an evening with an old friend—even if it did mean losing a little sleep before going to work—was too good to pass up.

"I'd ..."

Before Jennifer could finish her answer, a now-familiar voice interrupted.

"Miss Kent, I'm glad you stopped by this morning. I've been meaning to discuss a few changes I think should be made." Jarrod's voice was casual, almost as if he had no idea he had intruded on a private conversation, but the mischievous sparkle in his eyes told otherwise.

Glancing at David, Jarrod continued, unhurried. "I feel more happens on the swing shift than graveyard, so I want you to change shifts with one of the other guards. Also, weekends seem to be active, so why don't you starting taking a couple of weekdays off instead of Saturday and Sunday?"

As innocent as if he had just commented on the brisk autumn weather instead of turning Jennifer's entire schedule upside down, Jarrod turned and entered the main office area.

Sitting down at Andrea's desk, Jarrod leaned back in the chair and swung his feet atop the cleared surface as he waited for Jennifer. A smile crossed his face. With her temper, he knew she would not let this suggestion pass without giving her opinion. Jarrod drew in a deep breath. Maybe he was being a little overbearing, but the thought of her going out with any other man kindled feelings close to jealousy ... well, maybe not jealousy, mused Jarrod; maybe he was just being protective. Protection! That thought brought an even broader grin. Could it be David he was protecting?

The sound of the back door slamming shut told him trouble was on its way.

"I thought you wanted to discuss the matter with me!" Jennifer fought to control the tight rein she was trying to keep on her temper. The Cheshire grin spreading across Jarrod's suntanned face, devastating under any other circumstances, only kindled her irritation. "Seems to me you've already made your decision."

"Well, I guess you could say I've made up my mind about several issues." A mysterious gleam sparkled deep within his dark eyes.

"And just what is that supposed to mean?"

"Never mind. I wouldn't mind spending the rest of the morning enjoying your company, but duty calls," Jarrod said with a lazy drawl.

Jennifer didn't bother responding as she turned and stormed out the door.

She had forgotten all about David as she strode toward the lunchroom and the only public telephone on the yard.

"Jennifer!" David caught her arm and spun her around. "Don't be so hard on Mr. Drake. He's doing what he thinks is best. And I must admit, most of the time he's right."

"Don't you start defending him, David. He had no right to order me to change everything around without even consulting me first. I'm in charge of the guards—not him!"

"Now, Jennifer, be reasonable. After all, this is his company, and he can do pretty much what he wants. Besides, why are you getting so mad? The problem's not that big."

"I'm sorry, David." Jennifer began to calm down as she listened to David's rationale. "I don't know. But that man just seems to rub me the wrong way."

David smiled. "At least we don't have two of you like that around here. Mr. Drake's more like his old self again. For a few days there, he was a real bear. Don't know what happened." David paused, as if by doing so he could solve the mystery. "He was fine, then one afternoon he went to Ukiah and the next day, boy! Nobody could do anything right. Then all of a sudden he's fine again. Guess I'll never understand people. Well, it looks like our date is off ... maybe later."

Jennifer was too irritated with Jarrod to notice the almost too-casual way David had sounded about their broken date.

"Listen, Jen, I'd better get to work. See you later." David shook his head as he walked into the mill's main building.

Jennifer continued on to the lunchroom, somewhat calmer than when she had first left Jarrod's office but still determined to put an end to his usurpation of her authority.

After dialing the number Lieutenant Edwards had given her, Jennifer waited for an answer at the other end of the line. Without giving the person answering the phone a chance to speak, Jennifer started talking. "Lieutenant Edwards, this is Jennifer Kent."

"Jennifer, it's so nice to hear from you. Is everything all right up there?" A note of concern edged his voice.

"Yes, but Jar ... Mr. Drake just informed me that he wants a change on the schedule. I'm to work four to midnight and weekends. I thought I was in charge of scheduling when people are to work?"

She heard a slight pause before the lieutenant answered. "You are in charge, Jennifer, to a degree. But any change Mr. Drake wants to make in our operation is up to him. After all, it is his mill, and he is paying the bill."

Jennifer sighed as she thanked the lieutenant for his time and promised to try and make the best of the situation.

"He told you that since I'm paying the bill, this mill will be run my way, didn't he?"

The deep voice coming from behind her startled Jennifer, causing her to drop the receiver she had been clutching. She didn't need to turn around; she would have recognized that deep, velvety voice anywhere.

"That's what he said, Mr. Drake." Jennifer's honey-toned voice dripped with undisguised sarcasm. Her defiant stance was unapologetic.

With a firm but gentle grip, Jarrod's hands closed around her upper arms and turned her around to face him. Jennifer refused to look at his face, preferring to gaze at the buttons on the shirt stretched across his chest as he took in a deep breath before he spoke.

"Jennifer." Jarrod's voice was calm and patient, as if he were speaking to a small child. Cupping her chin in his hand, he forced her to look at his face. "This *is* my mill, and no matter who you work for, as long as you are here to do a job, you will do it my way. The sooner you understand that, the better the job will go for both of us."

"Yes, Mr. Drake, I understand. Now unless you have another matter to discuss with me, I have a job to do." Jennifer did not wait for him to dismiss her but turned out of his hold and walked through the door into the crisp morning air.

The next few days proved harder than she had anticipated. As if adjusting to a new schedule weren't enough to cope with, the newness of the job was being replaced by boredom in some of the guards. Jennifer saw one person quit without notice, and a couple of others simply did not show up for their assigned shifts. The shortages left all the staff with the added responsibilities of covering extra shifts until new replacements could be found.

After working for several days without a break, Jennifer entered the main office area at the end of a sixteen-hour double shift. The outer office was quiet since the regular coffee session had been moved to the comfort of Jarrod's office.

"What are you still doing here?" Jarrod asked with a surprised look on his face as Jennifer walked in to place the evening's reports on his desk.

"One of my men didn't show up last night, and no one else was able to work."

"You look like you could use a cup of coffee. What do you take in it?" Jarrod asked as he rose from his chair.

"Just black, thank you," Jennifer replied, too weary to make even the simplest decision.

"Move over, boys, and let the lady sit down," Jarrod ordered the group of men gathered about his office.

They provided a spot for her on the long, dark leather couch that matched the chair Jarrod had just vacated. She sank into the plump cushion, allowing herself the pleasure of a moment's rest before she had to complete her tasks for the remainder of the shift. It made no difference that after the past weeks she had at last been invited into the inner circle of Drake Lumber; she was too tired to enjoy the small victory they had awarded her.

As she glanced around the spacious office, she admired the natural beauty of the room, from the tongue-in-groove wooden walls, darkened with age, to the beautiful array of wildlife pictures adorning one complete wall.

A built-in bookshelf that took up the wall opposite Jarrod's desk contained a vast selection of information dealing with every phase of the lumber industry, from forestry to marketing the finished product. The wall behind the owner's desk featured a floor-to-ceiling picture window that looked out over most of the mill yard. A thick layer of dark brown carpeting added the finishing touches of luxury to this room, a contrast to the reserved atmosphere of the wooden flooring in the outer office.

Jennifer was surprised to see a well-used Bible on the corner of Jarrod's desk. She had never pictured a man as successful as he was would ever feel the need to rely on anyone other than himself.

Jarrod's tall form cast a shadow over Jennifer as he stood in front of her and handed her a cup of strong-smelling coffee. The lines of concern that etched the corners of his dark eyes and the warm touch of his hands as they closed over hers to steady her tired limbs sent unfamiliar emotions seeping through her exhausted body.

Jennifer became afraid that Jarrod would see the confusion she was feeling. She sipped at the steaming coffee to avoid his intense gaze. She was not surprised when the coffee proved much too hot to drink. She didn't really want to drink it anyway. Waiting for it to cool would allow her a chance to rest a little longer. After setting the coffee cup on the corner of the desk, Jennifer leaned back and rested her head against the back of the couch, trying to avoid Jarrod's scrutiny. A sincere smile touched her expressive lips as she listened to the cheerful bantering of the various department heads and felt the warmth of the morning sun radiating through the wall of glass behind Jarrod. She was far to weary to notice the pair of coal black eyes that never strayed from her face.

"Come on, you're going home," Jarrod stated with a note of irritation as he rose from behind his desk and closed the brief space between them to grip her elbow and pull her to her feet, the swiftness of his action taking everyone by surprise. Jennifer was whisked past the astonished onlookers and out the front door before those present were conscious of what was taking place.

"I'll be back soon," Jarrod called over his shoulder as they passed Andrea on the walkway to the parking lot.

"What are you doing?" Jennifer protested at his unusual behavior.

"I'm taking you home where you can get some rest," Jarrod stated as a matter of fact, opening the passenger's door of a late-model luxury vehicle parked close to the front of the building. "Now get in! As tired as you look, you'd probably fall asleep driving yourself home. You have no excuse for this, Jennifer. If you don't have dependable people working for you, then get rid of them and find someone who is willing to do the work. Do I make myself clear?"

Jennifer shook her head that she understood and could feel tears of frustration and exhaustion welling up in her eyes as Jarrod circled the car and slid into the seat behind the steering wheel.

Jarrod took a tissue from the glove compartment and handed it to his passenger and then brought the powerful engine to life.

After wiping the sprinkling of tears from her face, Jennifer laid her head on the back of the seat and let the soft comfort of the vehicle wrap itself around her weary and tense body. The soothing melody of a concerto emanating from the stereo beckoned her to a land of rest and dreams. So complete was her relaxed state that the halted motion of the car failed to awaken her sleeping form. A smile touched her lips as the gentle caress of a man's hand made it presence felt on her cheek. The dream was so real that Jennifer opened her eyes and sighed. At once realizing Jarrod was the source of her pleasure, Jennifer bolted upright in the seat and met his teasing eyes.

"I was beginning to think I'd never be able to make you smile," he chided with gentleness.

The softness and tenderness Jennifer saw in his face and eyes were almost enough to wipe away all the resentment she had come to hold against him—almost, but not quite.

"How long have we been here?" Jennifer questioned to hide her wayward thoughts.

"About five minutes." Jarrod's answer was causal and unhurried.

"Why didn't you wake me up?"

"Because you looked so contented and happy just the way you were."

"Don't you think you'd better be getting back to work?" Jennifer retorted, feeling very self-conscious for having allowed herself to become so at ease in his presence.

"That's one of the advantages of owning one's own company; I can set my own hours. You wouldn't be trying to get rid of me, would you?" Jarrod's voice remained gentle and teasing as he sat leaning against the driver's door. "But you're the one who should be leaving and getting some rest." Jarrod sighed as he opened his door and exited the car.

Jennifer watched as he circled the automobile to open the passenger's door, her mind more confused than ever by this man who seemed to be able to extract so many emotions from her. She took the hand he offered her as she stepped out of the vehicle, looked up into his face, and offered a lame thanks for the ride home.

Jarrod continued to hold her hand as his thumb caressed her soft skin, sending tingling waves of excitement through her body. It was silly for something as simple as someone holding her hand to be having this effect on her; Jennifer scolded herself for her reactions.

"It was no trouble at all," Jarrod said as he bowed from the waist in a chivalrous manner.

Jennifer withdrew her hand now that she was standing firmly on the ground and retreated to the safety of her own home without even looking back. She had no wish for the mire of confusion rushing through her to disturb the otherwise calm façade she was attempting to present.

Standing against the kitchen door, she waited for the car to pull away from the driveway as the sound of her own heartbeat thundered in her ears. Once the sound of the powerful motor faded, Jennifer finally felt calm enough to move away from the support of the sturdy wooden door.

"Jennifer, was that Jarrod's car in the driveway?" Mrs. Kent called from the living room.

"Yes, Mom, he brought me home," Jennifer said, pausing on the staircase.

"Is everything all right, dear?" Mrs. Kent came to the foot of the stairs and looked up at her daughter.

"Yes, he just felt I might be too tired to drive myself home."

"That's so like him, always thinking of others." Mrs. Kent smiled as she turned and walked back into the living room.

Jennifer shook her head as she climbed the remainder of the stairs. Too much was not as it appeared to be. Her troubled heart ached for peace and order in her life, and Jarrod Drake only seemed to be making things more complicated than they already were.

Jennifer fell asleep almost as soon as she crawled into bed, but it was a restless, troubled sleep. A smiling, benevolent face alternating with a stern determined one penetrated her dreams, and both of them bore a striking resemblance to Jarrod Drake.

The room was pitch black when she stirred from her slumber. When she reached for the alarm clock, Jennifer panicked at the late hour.

"It can't be! Mom, why didn't you call me? I'm late for work!" Jennifer yelled as she tried to hurry and dress for work.

"Because Jarrod called this afternoon and said to let you sleep. He said he'd made arrangements with the other guards and that you were to take at least two days off," Mrs. Kent said as she entered the younger woman's room.

A mixture of relief and irritation flooded over her. It would be nice to get the much-needed rest, and a couple of days off would be appreciated, but again Jarrod had intervened into her area of responsibility without asking her opinion.

Jennifer puttered around the house the next day, doing a few of the chores she had been putting off. Early that evening, however, the ringing of the telephone interrupted the tranquility of the day. Jennifer listened as her mother picked up the receiver.

"Hello." Mrs. Kent listened and then glanced in her daughter's direction. "Yes, she's here. Just a minute, Jarrod, and I'll get her."

As she held the phone out for Jennifer, Mrs. Kent didn't seem at all surprised that Jarrod could be calling for her daughter.

"Hello." Jennifer spoke with reserve, unsure why Jarrod would be calling.

"Jennifer, I hope you have been able to get some rest." His voice sounded concerned about the state of her wellbeing.

"Yes, thank you."

"Good! If you have no plans for tomorrow, I'd like you to accompany me to the Independent Mill Owners' meeting in Eureka. One of the items we'll be discussing is the security for our mills, and I'd like your input."

Jennifer bit her lip. The thought of spending the whole day with Jarrod was almost more than she was able to endure. Then again, here was a chance to express some of her ideas for improving the security service.

"Okay. What time is the meeting?" Jennifer questioned after a brief pause.

"It's a luncheon meeting so should start about noon. Why don't we leave here about eight o'clock, and that should give us plenty of time to get there? Some of the wives will be there too, and most of these people are old friends, so dress up a little bit. In other words, no jeans. See you tomorrow." The phone went dead.

"Why did I do that? Now the man is telling me how to dress!" The telephone receiver reverberated as Jennifer threw it back in its holder.

The following morning was a typical early fall morning in the patchwork of small valleys of the California coast range. The fog was so thick you couldn't see a block away, but it would burn off well before mid-morning. Jennifer was surprised at how peaceful her sleep had been during the night, unbothered by the prospect of the day that lay ahead. As she gazed out the upstairs window of her bedroom, she mused at how this morning was like so many others she had looked upon from the same window as she was growing up, yet this day already seemed different, like something special was just beyond the mist. Shaking her head at her overactive imagination, she turned from the window. She was a little surprised when she found herself taking special care with her appearance in preparation for the day's events.

Jarrod arrived right at eight o'clock. Jennifer's mother admitted him into the living room before informing her daughter of his presence.

As Jennifer reached the top of the staircase, she stopped short, surprised by the image before her. She had never seen Jarrod in anything but the jeans and casual shirts he wore to work and had never bothered to picture him any other way. She was amazed at how good he looked in a suit and tie. He stood with an arm resting on the banister, the other on his waist, having brushed his unbuttoned dark suit jacket back to reveal his shirt stretched to accent his broad chest that tapered into a taut abdomen. The black slacks only hinted at the sinewy thighs they concealed.

Jarrod lifted his eyes and surveyed the female form descending the stairs toward him. The straight lines of her gray woolen shirt glided softly over her willowy hips and thighs, the deep slit of the front of the skirt only offering glimpses of the shapely legs beneath. The black wool and velvet blazer set atop the feminine softness of her silken blouse offered just the correct touches of business and womanliness to set her apart from others of her sex. Only the slightest hint of admiration flickered in his eyes before he managed to draw a veil over his emotions.

"Thelma, I'd say you managed to raise a very unusual daughter there; she believes in being prompt." Jarrod spoke to Mrs. Kent, but his eyes never strayed from Jennifer.

"Chauvinist!" Jennifer muttered as she walked to the hall closet and removed her coat. Jarrod took the garment from her arm and held it open for her to slip into. As if on cue, they both glanced at their reflection in the hall mirror. Jennifer was astonished at the becoming appearance they made as a couple. Breaking their shared silence, Jennifer reached for her hat, which was resting on the table. Just as she started to place it in position on her head, Jarrod took it from her hand.

"Why hide that beautiful head of hair under a hat?" he remarked as he returned the hat to the table.

He's doing it again, Jennifer fretted to herself as she bit her lip in irritation. Picking up her soft leather gloves and purse, Jennifer closed the small space to where her mother was standing and gave her a brief hug.

"We shouldn't be too late," Jennifer promised.

"I won't worry; you'll be in good hands." Mrs. Kent smiled at Jarrod, pleased with her daughter's companion.

Jennifer turned to Jarrod and informed him she was ready to leave. Her mother's high opinion of him did little to alter her views of this man. As he opened the door for her, she picked up the hat and walked with a dare in her stride past his silent form to the vehicle waiting in the driveway. She failed to notice the smile of amusement that brightened his face or the wink he tossed in her mother's direction.

The two rode in silence through the thick valley fog and were soon traveling up the steep ribbon of highway that crossed the ridge surrounding their valley home. As the road leveled at the top of the hill and they reached the sunshine of Inspiration Point, Jennifer peered past the driver toward the fog-shrouded valley. This early-morning scene always reminded her of a bowl of fluffy whipped cream, with the surrounding hills forming the circumference of the bowl.

As if reading her mind, Jarrod whispered so as not to break the spell of the moment. "It's beautiful, isn't it?"

At least this was one subject they did agree upon—the beauty and tranquility of their valley.

With each passing curve, Jennifer felt the tension flowing from her body. The smoothness of the ride provided by the expensive automobile and the expertise of the driver all combined to make the long drive out to State Highway 101 a pleasant experience. Jarrod was a man confident in his own abilities, and he felt no need to impress her with how fast he could drive, as a majority of her previous escorts had done, but then that was also part of her high school days almost a lifetime ago. Jennifer studied the serene profile of her companion and found herself experiencing pride at being in his company, which she had never felt with any other man. She felt an undercurrent of excitement about him but also a peacefulness she found comforting.

The soothing music on the stereo only added to her feelings of contentment despite her former misgivings concerning Jarrod Drake. The mellow surroundings eliminated any urgent need for conversation. They were both content to dwell on their own thoughts.

Once they arrived at Highway 101 and headed north, the traffic picked up, but at least the hordes of campers and vacationers that jammed this road during the summer months had thinned out. It was early enough in the day for the low-lying pockets and stretches of road along the Eel River to still be making a last-ditch effort to cling to their nightly fog cover. The rest of the road was already bathed in the rich warmth of early fall sunshine.

As they dipped into a dense pocket of fog, Jarrod ventured to break the silence.

"Places like this always make me feel so much closer to God. The redwoods remind me of His greatness. The fog closes off the rest of the world, and it's only Him and me."

Jennifer offered no comment as she glanced out the car window and shuddered at the loneliness the misty scene evoked in her.

"I was surprised that you weren't at church Sunday," Jarrod continued, attempting to draw Jennifer out of her silence.

Jennifer shrugged her shoulders. "After getting off work at midnight, I really didn't feel like coming. I don't have weekends off anymore, remember?"

"Ouch! I guess I had that one coming. I seem to remember that you were very active in youth activities when you were younger."

Jennifer was surprised by his statement because he was at least ten years older than her, and by the time she was in her teens, Jarrod had already left the valley for college.

Noting her reaction, Jarrod smiled. "Mom and Dad had the local paper sent to me at school, and your name was always in it for one activity or another at church."

"People sometimes grow up and change." Bitterness coated her terse words.

"Sounds like someone has a chip on her shoulder and is blaming God for some injustice she feels has been committed against her."

"If God exists!"

"Jennifer! You don't doubt that!"

"I don't know what I believe anymore." Jennifer leaned her head back against the headrest and released a sad sigh. As if to end the conversation, she turned her head back to the uninviting countryside they were passing. At times she didn't know what she believed. She was afraid to acknowledge a personal God and just as afraid to deny His existence.

Jennifer's statements had also cast a shadow across the sunshine she had brought to Jarrod's heart. For the first time since their encounter beside the highway, he realized that maybe God had other plans for their relationship than those he had envisioned. Sending a silent prayer toward heaven, Jarrod asked God for guidance and understanding through the dense gray clouds that had engulfed them.

The miles passed in silence as both Jennifer and Jarrod remained deep in their own thoughts.

As they passed the high water mark of the December 1964 flood that had inundated the area so savagely, Jarrod remarked, almost to himself, "It's hard to imagine the water ever reaching this height."

Jennifer threw him a look of astonishment.

"This is the second time today you've looked at me like that. What's the matter?" Jarrod quizzed, puzzled by her actions.

"Nothing! It's just I was thinking the exact same thought," Jennifer answered, a little shaken that this had happened twice in the same day.

Jarrod chuckled. "That's a skill I'm going to have to perfect."

Jennifer could feel the color rising in her cheeks as she shifted in her seat.

"Not only is she on time, but she also blushes. Looks like I'm traveling with a very old-fashioned girl here." Jarrod's voice sparkled with laughter as he teased his companion.

"Were you living in Covelo during the flood?" Jennifer asked, attempting to steer the subject of the conversation away from herself and glad the tension that had sprung up between them was decreasing.

"Yes, but I was too young to remember much other than from the stories I heard. My dad said it was the only time the valley was completely cut off from the outside world. The bridges crossing the Eel and its tributaries had either been washed out or were bent so bad you couldn't drive across them. My folks took in several people who were stranded in the valley. It was over four weeks before some of those folks were able to get home. I'm sure it wasn't a very merry Christmas for a lot of people that year." Jarrod paused and looked at Jennifer to make sure his dissertation was not boring his listener.

"Go on," Jennifer encouraged, fascinated by the story and the storyteller.

"Mom and Dad made the rounds of all the mill employees to make sure they were safe. I remember Dad saying they used quite a lot of the mill's heavy equipment to help get things back in order again. Most of the flood waters that did damage in this area"—Jarrod pointed to some of the lower lying areas along the highway as they passed by—"didn't come from the rains or melting snow but from a huge mud and debris dam across the river up around Meyers Flat. When it broke, most of this area was hit with a wall of water and debris that wiped out just about everything in its path."

"How did people get supplies and medical help?" Jennifer found herself caught up in the drama and danger of another time as she listened to Jarrod talk.

"The government used military transport planes and helicopters to bring in most of what was needed. They even fed the cattle out of the planes. We were without power for days at a time. It really brought out some of the best in people, and they opened their homes and hearts to those who needed help. As always, some hoarded groceries and the like, but thank God they were few and far between."

Jennifer's heart swelled with pride as she pictured Jarrod sharing his belonging with strangers and those less fortunate. Even as a child, she imagined he had possessed a maturity far beyond his years. She could see why Ezra had liked Jarrod; they were very much alike, even in their unshakeable faith in God.

"I hope you don't mind driving up here today, but this happened to be the week the company plane was scheduled to go in for its yearly maintenance checkup," Jarrod said as they neared the city limits of Eureka, the largest city between the bay area and the Oregon border.

"No, I don't mind at all. In fact, it's been pleasant to be able to enjoy the scenery for a change. If Mom and I come up this way, I have to do the driving, and you don't get much of a chance to see the sights that way."

"Next time we come up, we'll have to fly. It is breathtaking country from the air. If it's during the first few months of the year, you might enjoy flying out over the ocean, and maybe we could catch some of the whales as they come down the coastline."

"I'd like that very much," Jennifer replied. The possibility of a future trip sounded interesting, but the prospect of the two of them sharing more time together was even more pleasurable.

CHAPTER

. . . .

5

. . . .

J arrod drove to the historic Eureka Inn, where the meeting was being held, without any problems. The sun had broken through the clouds, and the temperature had risen to a more comfortable warmth since their early-morning departure. Jennifer decided her coat was unnecessary, along with the gloves and of course, her hat. As they walked across the parking lot to the main entrance of the elegant building, Jarrod placed his arm around Jennifer's back and rested his hand on her waist. His gently possessive touch shot waves of searing pleasure the full length of her body. Her startled look was met with a quiet dare and promise that any attempt to protest would do her no good.

The main lobby of the inn was decorated with fine pieces of furniture that reflected a more refined and elegant era. It was easy to see why the inn had been chosen to provide housing for presidents and foreign dignitaries alike from time to time. The arrival of the handsome couple did not go unnoticed, and both the gentleman and his lady received glances of admiration from those they passed.

The mill owners' meeting was held in one of the smaller conference rooms, and it had already begun to fill as they made their way through the small clusters of people waiting for the activities to begin. Jarrod's hand never left Jennifer's waist as rounds of introductions were made to the various mill owners and their wives.

Many of the older gentlemen gave Jarrod winks and smiles of approval as he introduced them to Jennifer. The inference that she belonged to him began to grate on her nerves. The muscles of her neck and back grew taut and tense as her irritation increased.

"Would you like something to drink?" Jarrod bent to whisper in her ear.

Jennifer nodded, pleased to be left alone, if only for a few minutes. The tranquility of the ride had begun to fade, and her old hostilities were again surfacing. So great was her irritation that she failed to notice the frumpy, middle-aged man approaching her until he touched her elbow, causing her to jump with surprise.

"When I said be nice to Mr. Drake, Sergeant Kent, this isn't quite what I had in mind."

"I beg your pardon, just what is that supposed to mean?" The snide remark only added to her already-angered state. "Mr. Drake just invited me to this meeting to add my input concerning security matters at the mill." She glared at the poor excuse for a man and dared him to continue his insinuations.

"You must be a quick learner, Miss Kent."

"It seems to me Sergeant Kent would know what actions would improve the quality of the security service rather than those of us who are not working the daily shifts. Don't you agree, Lieutenant Edwards, was it?" Jarrod asked as he handed Jennifer a tall, frosty glass of iced tea topped with a fresh sprig of mint.

Jennifer was so angered by the lieutenant's accusations that her hands were trembling as she attempted to hold her glass. Noticing her difficulty, Jarrod took it from her and sat it on one of the tables prepared for the luncheon.

"I want you to meet someone," Jarrod announced, and taking Jennifer's hand in his own, he led her away from the older gentleman and toward another group of people, most of whom were about their own age.

"Jennifer, I'd like you to meet Bradley Evans. His family owns the largest Redwood mill in this part of the country. Because of his size, we call him the Giant of the North." Jarrod paused as he maneuvered Jennifer toward the mountain of a man who seemed to be the center of everyone's attention. "We were also roommates in college. Brad, this is Jennifer Kent, the sergeant of the mill's security force."

Jarrod released his hold on her hand and resumed his possessive grip on her waist. The smiles of friendship between the two men sprang from a long association and deep admiration of each other's accomplishments.

"I wondered why Jarrod changed his mind about the need for a security force at his mill; now I understand." Bradley's good-natured teasing was not lost as he clasped Jennifer's hand in both of his and made no secret of admiring the young woman standing before him.

"It's nice to meet you, Mr. Evans," Jennifer replied, embarrassed by Bradley's actions.

"Call me Brad, please."

"Brad, why don't you join us at our table?" Jennifer offered, not wishing to spend the entire meeting in Jarrod's company alone. Lieutenant Edwards had also managed to deposit himself at the table they had established as theirs. The combination of Jarrod and the lieutenant would have been more than she felt able to endure in her present state.

The president of the association announced that lunch was being served and requested that everyone take a seat. Both Brad and Jarrod reached for Jennifer's chair, and each stood with his hand on the back of her chair, refusing to give in to the other as Jennifer slid onto the chair and ignored the childish behavior of the two friends. Bradley beamed with amusement at some private joke he seemed to be playing on Jarrod. Lieutenant Edwards gave both men a look of irritation and made no attempt to enter any of the casual conversation that passed between the other diners seated at the table with him.

"Jarrod, would you please lead us in the invocation?" the president asked from the podium.

Jarrod rose, and his clear, rich voice rang out across the room full of diners. He spoke with a confidence and frankness associated with a close personal relationship with the Person to whom he was speaking.

Jennifer bowed her head and could almost hear her father as he, too, spoke to his Maker with the same earnestness Jarrod possessed.

The luncheon fare was excellent, from the green salad and clam chowder to the fresh Humboldt Bay halibut, a specialty of the inn. Despite the tempting quality of the meal, Jennifer was much too tense to enjoy the cuisine and spent most of the time toying with the food as it sat on the plate in front of her. Even the chocolate mousse proved uninviting.

As last, much to Jennifer's relief, the meal was over and the dishes were removed from the tables. The few minutes before the meeting began provided her time to refresh her sagging spirits. After excusing herself from the table, Jennifer made her way to the ladies' room through the small crowd of people congregating in the hallway.

Several other ladies had the same idea, and the little lounge area turned out to be quite crowded. As she stood near the wall, she could not help but overhear several of the conversations going on around her. She listened with growing interest to a couple of elderly ladies when she realized she and Jarrod were the subject of their discussion.

"I'm so glad to see Jarrod has finally found someone. I was beginning to worry about that young man."

"She's such a pretty little thing too. They do make a nice-looking couple."

"She reminds me of his mother, Rachel. You remember her, don't you, dear?"

"Of course I do. But they don't look anything alike."

"I didn't mean in looks. I meant in her quiet manner, yet there's strength in her too. You can just see it in the way she carries herself. My grandpa used to say what this country needed was 'Men to match its mountains and women to match its men.' I think that man has found his match."

Both women nodded in agreement as they finished their touchups and left the lounge. Jennifer walked to the mirror and gazed at her pale complexion.

A touch of blush still didn't take away the ashen color the ladies' conversation had painted on her cheeks. After taking out her brush, Jennifer began to brush her hair. Each stroke became more vehement the longer she thought of her name being linked with that of Jarrod Drake. All of a sudden, she stopped in mid-stroke.

Was it that she didn't like the idea of being considered a part of Jarrod's life, or was it that none of their gossip was true that really bothered her?

She could not deny the stirring of her innermost emotions whenever Jarrod was near, nor could she deny the physical excitement she felt as his slightest touch, but he had never indicated he felt anything for her. What if all her feelings were just her imagination? The thought of enduring more humiliation at his hands was more than her heart and spirit could bear.

Replacing the brush in her purse, Jennifer realized she was alone in the room and must return to the meeting. With a sigh of reluctance, she opened the door and walked out into the lobby.

"I'd begun to think you had gotten lost." Jarrod's voice came from behind her as he pushed away from the wall he had been leaning against.

"As you can see, I'm fine," Jennifer replied with an unnecessary sharpness. She watched as the flicker of what could have been pain flashed across those dark eyes that were fast becoming so dear to her.

"I'd say you were more than just fine. But the discussion of security matters is about to begin. So shall we return?" he asked, not expecting an answer as he took her elbow and moved in the direction of the conference room.

As they entered the room and were making their way back to their seats, the chairman of the conference announced the next item on the agenda.

Jennifer's eyes glanced at Lieutenant Edwards, and she caught the undeniable look of disgust on his face as he watched Jarrod once again hold the back of her chair until she was seated. Bradley had the same boyish grin on his face as he too watched the proceedings. From the first moment Jarrod had introduced the two of them earlier that morning, Bradley seemed to be enjoying some private joke or secret. Jennifer was puzzled by the reactions of both the men who were occupying the table with her.

"Mr. Jarrod Drake, from the Drake Lumber Company in Covelo, has requested permission to speak. Mr. Drake, the floor is yours."

Jarrod rose from his chair and picked up a few sheets of paper he had taken from his briefcase and laid the charts and graphs out on the table. Then he began to address the audience. In a clear and concise voice, he presented every idea Jennifer had bombarded him with, in her numerous reports over the past months. However, he had taken her suggestions further and broken down each concept, presenting cost analysis, liability factors, and savings in manpower and efficiency. The report he was presenting encompassed many hours of research, study, and consideration.

"In conclusion, the independent mills are becoming a dinosaur of the past, rapidly being devoured by the giants of the industry who want to eliminate all but their own kind.

We are fast becoming a rare breed whose need for protection is growing more imperative. Since the association banded together and acquired our present security service, we have not had one act of violence or harassment. Neither has any owner sustained any substantial loss of any type.

"All of the suggestions I have just presented to you this afternoon have been the direct results of the observations by the head of the security force at my mill, Sergeant Jennifer Kent. I just elaborated on them a little bit."

Jarrod held out his hand for Jennifer to join him as the assembly began to field a steady stream of questions, most of them of a routine nature, since the presentation had been so thorough.

Jarrod's hand once again rested around the feminine curve of her waist as they stood side by side for the brief discussion session.

"Mr. Drake, I compliment you on your report, but don't you think the security company knows best how to run its own operation?" Lieutenant Edwards's high-pitched voice rang out above the general clamor of the room.

Jennifer could feel the nerves in Jarrod's arm across her back tighten as he listened to the lieutenant's insinuation that he had questioned the company's ability to handle their responsibilities effectively.

"Lieutenant Edwards, if we had not been confident in your company's abilities, we would not have hired you to handle our contract. However, each individual mill has its own particular set of needs, and these must be taken into consideration. The only way to ascertain these special requirements is to become familiar with that specific mill, and those most capable of doing this are the people who work at that location. It is our intent to receive the best and most efficient service possible from your company in meeting our needs. The management of your organization is aware of our intentions and has agreed to implement our suggestions to the best of their ability. If they have not seen fit to convey this information on to you, then that is between you and your employer and has nothing to do with us. Do you have any other questions I might help you with, Lieutenant Edwards?"

Edwards glared with hostility toward the awesome figure standing only a few feet in front of him. After a brief moment, the officer excused himself from the table and took up a stool at the bar near the back of the meeting room.

Jennifer was both amazed and proud of the presentation Jarrod had delivered and also of the way he had dismissed Edwards's attempt to undermine his objectives and expertise in delivering the report. At the end of the question-and-answer session, Jennifer caught Jarrod's smile of approval and felt a warm glow of pleasure flow through her body.

The rest of the meeting was long and tedious, and Jennifer felt a tremendous sense of relief when the speaker at last adjourned the meeting.

"Hey, Jar, a bunch of us are going to the Cookhouse for supper; want to join us before you start back?" Bradley spoke over the noise of scraping chairs and the general clamor that now filled the meeting room.

Jarrod looked at Jennifer and raised an eyebrow, silently seeking her opinion in the matter.

"Sounds like fun." Jennifer smiled at Bradley as she spoke for both of them.

"Good! If it had been left up to ol' Jarrod there, he'd have headed back for his little hole in the wall." Bradley grinned mischievously as he placed his arm around Jennifer's shoulder and pretended he didn't want anyone else to hear what he was about to say. "Did anyone ever warn you about this fellow over here?" He nodded toward Jarrod.

"Is there something you think I should know about?" Jennifer replied, enjoying the lighthearted atmosphere of the moment.

"Well, my dear," Bradley continued, "there's so much I could tell you, but it just might take a while. What are you doing next weekend?"

"Working, my dear friend," Jarrod interrupted as he removed Bradley's hand from Jennifer's shoulder. "For me!"

Bradley's face radiated the pleasure his teasing was causing. "Bet that was your idea," Jennifer heard him mutter under his breath to Jarrod as the small group walked through the front doors of the inn.

The late afternoon sky was a brilliant blue, with patches of fluffy white clouds drifting at a leisurely pace inland. A gentle breeze played tag with anything that would move.

"You know the way, Jarrod. We'll save you a place," Bradley called over his shoulder as the small group of friends headed for their respective vehicles.

Jarrod discarded his suit jacket and tie, holding them over his shoulder. He unbuttoned the top button of his expensive white shirt and rolled up the sleeves to reveal the deep, rich, suntanned skin of his forearms and a matching V-shaped patch at his throat. The fine growth of dark hair on his sturdy arms was barely visible where he had just unbuttoned his shirt and contrasted sharply against the brightness of the white shirt. Once again he took up his possessive hold on Jennifer's waist as they bade farewell to the few remaining couples. They were soon bringing up the rear of the caravan of cars headed across the waters of Humboldt Bay to the Samoa Cookhouse.

"Have you ever been here before?" Jarrod asked as they turned into the parking lot of the long, two-story, weathered building just up from the water's edge.

"No, but I've heard about it."

"I think you'll like it. The walls are covered with lots of photographs and pieces of equipment once used in the logging industry. The building itself was actually a cookhouse for the crews that worked the mills here. The cooks and waitresses lived in dorms upstairs. At that time in history the companies provided everything for their employees from housing, medical needs, meals, and of course, the company store."

"Sounds a lot like the way mining towns worked in the Appalachians."

"Actually it was, but most people don't realize that."

Jennifer enjoyed the meal and discovered that for the first time during the long day, she was actually hungry. Jarrod's knowledge of the history of this part of the country was fascinating. His friends were an entertaining, fun group of people, and the time passed way too fast.

The sun was drifting closer to the horizon as the sleek Lincoln Navigator pulled onto the highway and headed south along the edge of the bay.

Without warning, Jarrod turned onto a beach access road and then onto a rutty, seldom-used dirt road.

"Where are we going?" Jennifer demanded as Jarrod swerved to avoid one of the numerous potholes.

"This was too pretty to pass up," Jarrod said as he threw a roguish smile in her direction.

What little road she could see came to an abrupt end at a small turnaround large enough to accommodate maybe one or two vehicles at a time.

"Come on," Jarrod challenged as he removed his shoes and socks and began to roll up his trouser legs.

"But I've got heels and nylons on," Jennifer protested as she looked at her meticulous attire.

"Well, take your shoes off, and I'll buy you a new pair of stockings if those get ruined."

Still not sure about just what was going on, Jennifer removed her shoes as Jarrod walked around the car and opened the door, offering her his hand as she exited the car.

The breeze had picked up and had a slight chill to it, but the sand still felt warm under her feet as she followed Jarrod's lead up the narrow trail through the small dunes and beach grass.

The golden rays of the sun glistened across the gentle wave of the water as the couple topped the last dune and stood just above the smooth sand of the water's edge. Only the screech of a gull and the constant ebb and flow of the Pacific Ocean broke the silence around them as they paused and watched the timeless beauty of the scene.

"When my dad died, this is the only place that seemed to help me accept what had happened. Watching the waves helped remind me that no matter what happens, life goes on."

Jennifer moved away from Jarrod's side and sat on the smooth surface of a large piece of driftwood. Obviously this place was very special to Jarrod, and it made her a little uneasy that he had chosen to share it with her.

Jarrod continued, "I often walked down the beach, and when I turned around and would see only one set of footprints in the sand, it always reminded me of the poem, 'Footprints in the Sand,' and I knew God was always there with me and He would help me through my grief.

"Jennifer, I know what you're going through, but you can't keep all your feelings inside or go on blaming God for what happened. As much as we love or value someone, one day we're going to know some kind of grief, whether from disappointment or loss. We wouldn't know sorrow if we hadn't experienced love and joy."

"Then maybe it's better not to love anything or anyone if all it means is pain and grief." Jennifer's voice was husky with emotion.

"You can't wrap yourself in a void and not touch or be touched by other people. Even a hermit comes in contact with others from time to time."

"But Dad's death was so sudden ..."

"Jennifer, no one ever knows when they are going to leave this world; you know that."

"If only I'd had a chance to talk to him before he died. Jarrod, there were so many things I needed to say to him." Jennifer could feel the tears welling up in her eyes as she remembered their last bitter conversation, all the hateful, hurting things she had said and never really meant.

"We all have regrets—stuff we wish we had or hadn't said, goals we wanted to accomplish. All we can do is make the most of every minute we're given."

"You make it all sound so easy." Jennifer paused, unsure whether to press on. "Jarrod ... was your dad sick long before he passed away?"

Jarrod paused before he spoke. "I don't remember Dad ever being sick a day in his life." Picking up a small pebble, he sent it sailing along the receding surf before continuing. "We'd had a meeting at the mill one evening, and Dad left to go home. He was excited about the new plans we had been working on," he said, taking a deep breath, his voice faint above the pounding water. "That was the last time I saw him alive ... His car was hit head-on by a drunk driver, and he was killed instantly."

"Oh, Jarrod, I'm so sorry. I didn't know. I just assumed he had been ill."

Jarrod reached for her hand and clasp it firmly in his as he pulled her to her feet. "Come; walk on the beach with me."

Both were deep in their own thoughts as they walked hand in hand down the isolated stretch of beach. Their shared losses formed a bond whose roots were far too deep to discuss or question.

Time was marked only by the lengthening shadows and reddening sky as the sun began to dip out of sight in the horizon. The wind became more brisk and had picked up a chill that sent shudders down Jennifer's arms as it whipped across the surf.

"Maybe it's time we headed back." Jarrod wrapped his arms around her slender form and held her close. "Thanks for coming here with me, Jennifer."

"Thank you for sharing it with me,"

The trek back along the seashore was a comfortable mingling of sounds; wind, surf, seagulls, and an occasional comment. The whole world seemed at peace for those few moments Jennifer shared with Jarrod on that beautiful stretch of sand.

"Jennifer, if you ever feel like talking, I'll be more than willing to listen. Would you please remember that?"

Jarrod was so serious, and the earnestness of his request touched her deep within her heart.

"I'll remember."

The approaching darkness closed around them as they left the bright lights of the outskirts of the city behind and were once again surrounded by the clusters of giant redwoods that lined the narrow ribbon of concrete and asphalt they were traveling on.

The smooth ride of the elegant automobile, the fluid skill of the driver, and the late hour beckoned Jennifer to the comforting safety of sleep, to which she easily succumbed.

She had no recollection of how long she remained asleep, but the pause in motion of the vehicle awakened her drowsy senses.

"Where are we?" Jennifer asked after failing to recognize any of the surrounding countryside. She felt a little uneasy because, for the first time in a very long time, she had been able to sleep in a deep restful state and had not been plagued by the dreams that had haunted her for the past several months.

Jarrod could send her emotions into a state of turmoil in a moment, but he was also able to provide peace and comfort by just being near.

"Just north of Leggett. Something must have happened up ahead. Caltrans have their road crews out, and traffic is being stopped." Jarrod seemed unconcerned about the delay, and Jennifer found that she, too, was not dismayed by the situation.

A state highway employee appeared out of the fog and began working his way from car to car. Jarrod rolled down his window as the man reached them.

"There's been a rockslide about a mile up the road. We're working on clearing it now, but it may take a couple of hours to get the road open again. You folks can either turn around or wait here."

Jarrod thanked the man and turned to Jennifer. "We might as well just wait it out here, if you don't mind. The nearest motels are probably full unless we go all the way back to Eureka."

Jennifer nodded in agreement. Taking her coat from where it lay over the seat between them, she slipped off her shoes, tucked her legs under her, and curled up beneath the warmth of the coat, intending to ignore Jarrod and attempt to snatch a few more hours of much-needed sleep.

Much later Jennifer sensed Jarrod's eyes watching her, and as she opened her own, she found him facing her with his back resting against the driver's door.

"You really shouldn't sleep that way, you know; it's much too tempting," he announced with a low drawl.

Jennifer looked at her position and saw that her whole body was quilted by her coat, and only her head was left uncovered.

"Shouldn't sleep how?"

"With your lips parted like that; they're much too inviting."

"I'll remember that the next time I fall asleep when you're around."

"Does that mean you'll be sleeping with me again sometime?" Jarrod replied suggestively.

Even in the dark, Jennifer could sense the mischievous sparkle in his dark eyes as he teased her. She could also feel the burning glow of her own cheeks as her thoughts followed the same direction.

"That's not what I meant at all, and you know it! What time is it?" Jennifer asked, attempting to steer the conversation and her own thought to safer ground.

"Almost three o'clock."

"In the morning!"

"Yes, are you afraid people will talk about you spending the night with me?" Jarrod continued his teasing, enjoying her discomfort.

"No!" she lied. "It's just that we both have to work tomorrow and won't get much rest tonight. Besides, I'm sure Mom is worried sick by now."

"I called your mother a while back and told her what was going on, so she's fine. But speaking of rest, Sleeping Beauty," he noted, "why don't you drive the rest of the way home and let me get some sleep?"

"Me drive?"

"I know you know how to drive!"

"Yes, but this?" Jennifer asked, holding out her hands to indicate the expensive automobile.

"It drives just like any other car, maybe just a little easier," he stated rather matter-of-factly as he opened the driver's door and walked to the passenger's side of the car. Jennifer threw her coat into the backseat, searched for her shoes, and waited for Jarrod to open her door before she stepped out of the vehicle and walked to the driver's side of the vehicle and the seat her boss had just vacated. "How do I adjust the seat?"

Jarrod placed one arm across the back of the seat and reached across between Jennifer and the steering wheel to indicate which buttons controlled what functions. His arm remained stretched across the back of the seat, and Jennifer could feel the muscles in her body tighten.

Jarrod sensed it too as he began to massage the back of her neck. "Just relax. I assure you, driving this car is no different than any other."

"Jarrod, please don't do that!" Jennifer almost whispered her plea as she felt the blood pulsating through her veins and her limbs growing weaker with each succeeding caress of his fingers.

"Does it bother you? If it does, I'll stop." His voice held only a trace of honesty as he continued to stroke the soft lines of her neck.

The lights of the long line of cars ahead of them began to appear, and Jennifer was spared the discomfort of answering his query. They would soon be on their way again. Jarrod was having too much effect on her senses for her to remain uncommitted to his gentle bombardments of attention for much longer.

After the car resumed its previous momentum, Jarrod reclined his seat, and Jennifer soon heard soft, rhythmic breathing emanating from his sleeping form. His sleep helped ease some of the pent-up tension that had kept her from relaxing for the past hour. When she finally turned onto the Covelo Road, Jennifer felt more at ease and confident of herself than she had during most of the trip.

The lateness of the hour, the release of her taut nervousness, and the quiet surroundings of the interior of the Navigator all combined to induce her into a trance-like state. She went through the motions of driving but was not fully aware of what was occurring around her.

A quick flicker of movement along the side of the road caught her attention but not soon enough to catch the second object as a small doe darted in front of the vehicle. Her reactions were instinctive as she swerved to avoid hitting the deer, but she was unable to prevent a collision with a large rock outcropping on the side of the road. The sudden jerking motion of the vehicle awakened Jarrod just in time to brace for the abrupt impact with the ledge.

Jennifer failed to hear Jarrod's question as she bolted from the car and ran to survey the damage.

"I didn't mean to ... I'm so sorry ... please forgive me ... I'm so sorry ... your beautiful car," Jennifer sobbed as she stared at the crumpled fender of the Navigator.

By the time Jarrod reached her, she was crying uncontrollably. He took her in his arms and drew her close, resting her head on his chest. There he held her until the tears began to subside. Jennifer, in turn, wrapped her arms around his waist and drew strength from his mere presence.

"Everything's all right. Don't worry about the car; it can be repaired. Just thank God you're all right." He spoke gently and calmly against her hair.

Jarrod stroked Jennifer's upper arm and caressed her shoulders and neck until he cradled her face in his hands. He lifted her face toward his. Slowly and methodically, he began to kiss away the remnants of tears that had cascaded down her cheeks.

Jennifer felt herself being drawn into a whirlpool of new emotions and feelings as Jarrod lightly touched her lips. The anticipation was sweet agony, but Jarrod withheld the moment his lips fully captured hers until Jennifer felt she could not stand this exquisite torture a second longer.

A hint of uncertainty and doubt flashed across Jarrod's face, but the darkness of the night hid it from Jennifer. Only a flicker of hesitation could be noted before Jarrod finally, tenderly kissed the corners of her mouth and allowed their lips to meet. Savoring each touch, his lips spoke to her like a whisper that reached into her very soul.

For the first time in her life, Jennifer responded with an intensity and fierceness she didn't know she possessed. Sliding her hands up across his chest and shoulders, she entwined her fingers in the soft thickness of his dark hair.

Jarrod's breathing was ragged as he withdrew his lips from hers.

"Jennifer ..."

All of a sudden, they were both bathed in the harshness of a blinding spotlight.

"Is everything all right? Oh, Mr. Drake, I didn't recognize you," came a faceless voice from behind the light.

"Everything's okay. We just had a little accident," Jarrod replied as he maintained his embrace on Jennifer. She turned her head into his shoulder to escape the severe intensity of the offensive light.

"Do you need some help?" the emerging form asked.

"I think if we pull the fender away from the wheel, we can make it home," Jarrod informed the now-recognizable deputy sheriff.

As Jarrod released his hold on Jennifer, a shiver of cold engulfed her, not only from the loss of warmth from his body but also at the rapid descent her emotions were experiencing. Mistaking her trembling for the sudden exposure to the chilly night air, Jarrod shed his jacket and draped it over her shoulders.

Jennifer stood alongside the road and watched as the two men worked on the car, grateful for the few moments alone. Too much was happening too fast.

In a very short time, the damaged fender was straightened enough to drive, and Jarrod thanked the deputy for his help.

With his arm draped around Jennifer's shoulder, he led her back to the car. Taking up her seat on the passenger's side of the car, Jarrod rested his arm across the back of her seat, the console keeping them apart. *There are times when bench seats were really nice to have around,* Jennifer thought as she snuggled as close to Jarrod as she could. During rest of the trip home, Jarrod said very little, but Jennifer felt a peace and contentment her troubled heart had almost forgotten existed. At this moment, the two people in the silent vehicle surrounded by the darkness of night were all that mattered.

CHAPTER

Jennifer awoke the next morning to the radiant beauty of a crisp fall day. All nature beckoned her to partake in its splendor. In spite of the few hours of sleep she had managed the previous night, she felt more alive and happier than she had in a very long time. Throwing her clothes on with haste, she stepped out the back door of the Kent home and walked the short distance to the edge of town. Her soaring spirits were further enthralled by the crisp, sunbathed air and the beautiful splashes of the brilliant colors of the early fall foliage.

A creek bed ran meandering for miles through the floor of the valley and crossed the highway just outside of town. Jennifer climbed down the gentle, sloping incline of its banks and wandered along the rock pathway. Valley oak draped with Spanish moss and enormous bunches of mistletoe provided a natural barrier from the sights and sounds of the rest of the valley. Once in a while a small ground animal ran across the now-dry creek channel in front of her.

At times like this, Jennifer remembered the happiness she had experienced as a child—no worries, accepting as truth so many beliefs she had come to doubt as an adult.

It had been easy then to believe in an almighty God who would care for her and who she could turn to in time of trouble. But all that had changed. Where had He been when she had prayed so hard for her father to be allowed just a few more years? Where had He been when she needed comfort in her grief?

As Jennifer turned back toward town, the beauty of the countryside changed to loneliness with all her unanswered questions whirling around in her head. Even Jarrod was causing nothing but more confusion to her troubled heart. The fear of trusting her heart to someone, only to have it shattered, was not worth the small amount of pleasure his company might provide.

Jennifer resolved to reinforce the barrier she had erected around her wounded heart. With her shoulders held square, a more-determined and somber Jennifer Kent returned home.

"Jennifer, I'm surprised you're up already." Mrs. Kent looked surprised as the back door opened and her daughter walked into the kitchen.

"I couldn't sleep anymore, so I decided to take a walk."

"Is something troubling you, dear?" Concern and a slight frown creased the older woman's soft face.

"Nothing's wrong. Why do you ask?"

"You just haven't been yourself since you came back home ... like something's eating away at you. You know you used to confide in me, and we were able to work out a solution."

Jennifer twisted the edges of the tablecloth; her throat and mouth were dry as she thought of all that was troubling her, yet she felt unable to tell her mother any of it.

"Jennifer." Mrs. Kent pulled up a chair at the table next to her daughter and indicated for her to sit down also. "I never asked you or your father what happened that summer after your graduation. I just figured when the time was right, one of you would tell me." She paused to study Jennifer's face, now a pale ashen color, as she spoke. "Would you like to talk about it now?"

Jennifer swallowed hard, tears blurring her vision. "No."

She was surprised at the calmness of her own voice as she rose from the table and left the room. Now was not the time to talk about that summer that had changed her relationship with so many people she had known and her feelings about subjects she had once taken for granted.

Jennifer's mood had not improved much by the time she reported for work. All afternoon she had chastised herself for the sharpness she had used to respond to her mother's simple question, but she just couldn't talk about that summer—not yet.

As she headed out across the yard between the outlying buildings, Jennifer jumped at the blast of a pickup horn right behind her.

"Get in," Jarrod ordered as he reached across the seat of the pickup truck and opened the passenger side door. With a great deal of reluctance, Jennifer climbed into the cab and slammed the door, keeping her eyes straight ahead.

"Humph! Looks like somebody sure got up on the wrong side of the bed this morning," Jarrod commented as he maneuvered the pickup across the mill yard.

"As a matter of fact, I got up in a very good mood this morning, but things have just gone downhill since then."

"Want to tell me what happened? You might find I'm a very good listener." Jarrod's voice was quiet and sincere as he spoke, never taking his eyes off the dusty, bark-strewn ground in front of the truck.

Jennifer took in a deep breath and exhaled the fresh country air, scented with fresh-cut wood. She watched out the window as they passed the giant stacks of finished lumber and moved toward the decks of logs awaiting their turn at the saws.

"I just started thinking about too many painful memories, that's all."

"Have you talked with your mother about what you're going through since you got home, Jennifer?" Jarrod stopped the truck and watched for her answer.

Jennifer stared at the hands gripped together in her lap, remembering the hurt expression she had witnessed on her mother's face only a few short hours before.

"No, I just can't yet," she whispered.

"Jennifer, you know she loves you very much and only wants to help." Jarrod folded his large hands over hers, his touch both warm and strong.

"She would just say the same phrase she used to tell me when I had a problem: 'Have you talked to God about it?' I just can't do that, not now; maybe never."

"I want to show you something." Jarrod turned the pickup around and headed out across the open yard, heading for the back perimeter of the property, through a narrow cattle gate and onto a gravel road leading up the side of one of the hills surrounding the valley floor.

"Where are we going? I'm supposed to be at work."

"I don't think the boss will mind." Jarrod grinned boyishly.

The road was lined with weathered split-rail fencing, adding to the country feeling. About halfway up the hill on a gentle, grassy, tree-covered knoll overlooking the mill sat a simple but elegant two-story log house. The building site was well sheltered from the blustery gusts of wind that traversed the ridges of the hills before releasing their fury on the flat valley floor.

A small gasp escaped her throat as the house came into view. A wall of glass encased in heavy wooden beams formed a peak at the front of the house, its second story offering an unrestricted view of the mill and the valley stretching out before it. Decking and railings surrounded the entire structure. The wide steps leading from the driveway were an artistic blend of log beams, rock, and concrete edged with an abundant but well-tended expanse of ground cover.

Jennifer stared in disbelief at the setting before her. It was as if someone had captured in reality the house she had fantasized about for years.

"I'm so glad you approve. It's taken me several years to get this just the way I wanted it to look," Jarrod remarked with pride, mistaking her surprise for admiration.

Jennifer took in the entire scene and felt an ache in the region near her heart, as if yet another dream had just been shattered. This house couldn't belong to Jarrod Drake—not her dream house.

"Come on, I want to show you around." Jarrod took her hand and helped her out of the truck. Still keeping his hand around hers, he began to lead her toward a corral and barn area just down the hill from the house. As they approached, a large, muscular horse pranced toward them with an amazing amount of agility for an animal of its size.

Jennifer held back, keeping Jarrod safely between her and the unfamiliar, large animal as it playfully nuzzled Jarrod's shoulder, pushing him toward the empty grain bucket hanging on one of the posts of the enclosure.

The bond of friendship between the man and animal was evident as Jarrod stroked the powerful lines of the steed and proclaimed the many admirable qualities the horse possessed. As they neared the end of the fence, Jarrod gathered a couple of apples from a bucket alongside the small storage building adjacent to the corral, aptly tossing one to Jennifer.

"What am I supposed to do with this?" Jennifer questioned apprehensively as she looked at the overripe fruit she had barely managed to catch.

"Feed it to Lumberjack, of course." Jarrod grinned at her scowl of hesitation and uncertainty. "Don't worry; he won't bite."

"That's quite all right," Jennifer declined, politely handing the apple back to him. "Horses and I have an understanding; we don't like each other."

Jarrod refused to accept her explanation as he took hold of her wrist and forced the hand containing the apple toward the horse's mouth. With restrained effort, Lumberjack took the food offered him without so much as touching the delicate outstretched hand. Once the animal had devoured his snack, he gently nuzzled Jennifer's cheek, inducing a squeal of surprise from the recipient of his affection.

"I told you there was nothing to worry about. See? He even likes you." Jarrod chuckled at her response to this new experience.

"Where in the world did he get a name like Lumberjack?" Jennifer questioned as she reluctantly stroked the nose of the large horse standing before her.

"From me," Jarrod answered, enjoying the discomfort she was experiencing at his response. "Besides, what else would a lumberman call his horse?"

"Okay! I asked for that." Jennifer smiled in agreement to his teasing.

"Would you like to see the inside of the house now, or would you rather stay here and visit with Lumberjack?"

"No offense, Lumberjack, but I'd rather see the house." Jennifer offered the horse one last caress before turning from the corral to follow her host in the direction of the house.

Jarrod took her arm and rested it over his own in a way she found most pleasant. After unlocking the large wooden double doors and holding them open for her to enter, Jarrod waited as the beauty of the room overtook his guest.

Jennifer once again had the feeling that someone was playing a cruel joke and she was the butt of it as she looked around the spacious, open room. The interior of the two-story, open-beam-ceiling house was rich, in earthy colors of dark browns, tans, and creams. The house was not masculine as much as a delicate blend of nature and man.

The focal point of the living room was an oversized, natural river stone fireplace with a raised hearth. Several large pillows lay on the floor next to it, inviting guests and host alike to enjoy long, leisurely, intimate evenings basking in the radiant glow of a blazing fire.

A comfortable distance from the fireplace, a large beige sectional couch formed a semicircle around four matching ottomans. Throw pillows in shades of brown, tan, orange, and cream were scattered at random along the seating area. A long, high table butted against the back of the main section of the couch, providing the only table in that part of the room.

The opposite side of the open room was occupied by the dining room. An unobtrusive chandelier hung from the high ceiling over a large, intensely-polished wooden table and matching chairs that could accommodate a dozen guests, at least, for dinner. This was flanked to the left by a lighted china cabinet displaying a complete set of exquisite china and crystal.

Beyond the dining area was the kitchen that could be closed from view by wooden louvered doors. Wide, open stairs led to the balconied second story of the home. Jennifer could see the library and office area, but the rest of the second floor was obstructed from view.

The perusal took only a few seconds, but to Jennifer a lifetime of dreams and hopes were passing before her eyes. Of course, she saw minor differences from her dream house, but most of the changes Jarrod had made only improved the overall impression of the house.

"Well, are you just going to stand there all day or go on in?" Jarrod asked with laughter in his voice. "Lots of people have admired my home, but I don't think anyone has been quite as impressed as you seem to be. Considering I designed, built, and decorated the house myself, I take your admiration as a compliment."

"You decorated all of this?"

"Well, I will admit I didn't personally go to the stores and hand pick everything, but I did tell the interior decorator exactly what I wanted and had final approval on everything. You're not one of those women who thinks a man is all thumbs when it comes to anything that doesn't require brawn, are you?" Jarrod asked with amusement.

"No. It just surprises me a little, I guess. Although I'm beginning to think that nothing about you could be considered ordinary."

"I like the way you're thinking. It might also interest you to know that I can cook up a mean steak, and my chocolate mousse is magnificent," Jarrod finished with the flourish of a chef who had just created his crowning masterpiece.

Jennifer had to laugh at the antics of her host and realized once again how easy it was for her to relax when Jarrod was around. As she crossed the rich, deep chocolate expanse of carpet, she strongly wanted to indulge herself in the comfort and luxury of the room, but to do so would almost be a violation of her own secret daydreams.

The flickering of colored lights caught Jennifer's eye. Her attention was drawn to the uppermost part of the glass-and-beam front of the house. There, in meticulous detail, was a stained-glass mural depicting a forest scene complete with deer, streams, trees, and even a soaring eagle in the rich blue-and-white sky. Coming out of the forested area, a loaded logging truck heading toward a lumber mill completed the scene. Even from quite a distance, Jennifer could easily make out all the images depicted. The variety of colors seemed to dance and flicker to life as the setting sun played hide and seek with the passing clouds. Jennifer stood transfixed by the aura of colors that sparkled around the room.

"It really is beautiful, isn't it? Bradley made it for me after he saw my house plans." Jarrod's voice carried tones of awe as he, too, watched the display of lights flickering about them.

"Bradley?" Surprise registered in her voice that the giant of a man she had just met in Eureka was capable of such exquisite artistic workmanship.

"I'll have to take you to see the windows he did for the church he attends in Eureka. The one depicting the crucifixion always touches me beyond words." Jarrod paused, remembering the beauty of the scene before he continued. "Would you like to see the rest of the house or just stay here and watch the light show?" A smile spread across his handsome features, and amusement twinkled in those ebony eyes she found so riveting.

"I'm not sure I have time." Jennifer paused and looked at her watch more from nervousness than any particular need or desire to return to work.

"Come on, I'll put in a good word for you with the boss; he and I are on pretty good terms most of the time."

Taking her hand in his, Jarrod led the way toward the center of the large living room. Pausing at the foot of the wide staircase and resting his hand on the curved railing, he cocked his head to indicate they needed to go upward. "Upstairs we have my office and library, the master bedroom and bath—but I have a feeling you'd rather skip that part of the tour. So let's start with the kitchen."

This room too was especially large but was also well organized, with every major convenience one could wish for.

"This room speaks for itself," Jarrod remarked, still holding Jennifer's hand as he led her down the hallway and opened one of the closed doors.

The focal point of the guest bedroom was a large antique four-poster bed complete with a hand-quilted coverlet. On either side of the bed stood matching nightstands topped with delicate Victorian-style lamps and crocheted dollies. A massive dresser, rocking chair, and steamer trunk successfully completed the pioneer look of the room.

"This furniture all belonged to my grandparents. They were some of the first white people to settle this part of the country." A twinge of pride touched his face as he spoke.

"I didn't realize you were the sentimental type."

"I'm not really; I just appreciate quality workmanship and feel we can all learn from those who preceded us."

The long shadows of early evening were falling across the wooded area behind the house as Jarrod completed his brief tour and stepped out the back door onto the wraparound deck. The crispness of the country air felt good against their faces as they walked in silence down the steps and onto the gravel walkway. Suddenly Jarrod stopped short and pointed toward the edge of the wooded area.

Jennifer watched as a doe with twin fawns hesitantly made her way down the hillside. The agile creatures cleared the fences with such grace that neither of the onlookers made a sound for fear of frightening the beautiful creatures.

"Whenever I see the creatures of nature, I know beyond a doubt that there is a God." Jarrod spoke more to himself than to her, but Jennifer still found herself stiffen at his words.

"A god may have created the world, but I'm not so sure he's still around." The sharpness of her words came not from anger but from the pain and doubts she felt in her heart.

After turning her around to face him, Jarrod studied her before he spoke. "Why would God go to so much trouble making this world for us and then just go off and leave it alone? Don't you think He cares about what happens here? How could a parent give birth to a baby and then just up and leave it on its own?"

"Well, a baby is different; it needs help until it can take care of itself."

"And we don't need any help?"

"If He cares so much for us, then why doesn't He help us more? And why is He so unfair?"

"Jennifer, being fair is something man has come up with to get what he feels is right. God is just, and there's a big difference."

"Do you think it was just of Him to take my father's life ... or your father's, for that matter?" Jennifer pulled away from Jarrod, not wanting the comfort of his touch to temper her anger.

Jarrod stood silent, praying for the courage to say what Jennifer needed to hear.

"You've never once doubted or wondered about anything that's ever happened to you?" Jennifer asked, turning the focus back to Jarrod.

"Yes. Everyone has times when they are confused and deny the existence of God. Even those closest to Him, if you remember your Sunday school lessons, denied they ever knew Him. Jennifer, only you can find the peace you seek. Neither I nor anyone else can do it for you. I can tell you how I feel and show you where I get some of my answers, but for peace in your own heart you have to seek Him yourself."

"You make it all sound so easy."

"Jennifer, when you think about it, God did make it easy; we're the ones that make it complicated."

Jennifer broke off a blade of grass and methodically tore off one small piece at a time. *Jarrod made everything sound so simple, but hadn't she tried his way once? It just didn't work.*

Jennifer was pleased and surprised at Jarrod's honesty. He had freely admitted that he, too, had questioned his beliefs and even doubted at one time.

"This is my favorite spot in the early evening just before sunset." Jarrod spoke quietly, giving Jennifer a chance to calm her emotions and to guide the conversation in another direction if she so desired.

"I can see why." Jennifer was surprised at the distant sound of her own voice.

"There's a little spring just about at the tree line, and just about every night there will be at least two or three deer that come down to drink. Once in a while I'll see a bear or mountain lion. This is the spot where I took all of the wildlife photographs hanging in my office. It's also a good, peaceful place to unwind after a hectic day."

Placing his hand around her shoulders, Jarrod guided the thoughtful young woman down the gravel pathway toward the pickup.

"Thanks." With a voice as soft as a prayer, Jennifer turned to face Jarrod as he opened the door of the truck. Jarrod's lips were so close to her own that for a moment she thought—she hoped—he would take her in his arms and wipe away all her doubts, fears, and questions.

"What for, the tour?" His lips smiled as he spoke, but a deep concern still shadowed his eyes.

"Yes"—Jennifer paused before she continued—"and for not condemning me for my doubts."

"That's not my job. I just run a little ol' lumber mill."

"And do a very good job of it too."

The warmth of his smile helped take away the chill of the night on her flesh and some of the ice around her heart.

For several days after seeing Jarrod's beautiful home, Jennifer felt herself torn between anger, jealousy, and pride in the excellent way he had managed to bring into reality ideas she had only wished for and dreamed about.

Jarrod is a man who could move mountains if he wanted to. Jennifer smiled to herself as she pictured Jarrod's broad shoulders braced against a mighty mountain, trying to move it forcibly. *No! He wouldn't do it that way!* She stopped short. Jarrod would be practical and realistic. He would move it one piece at a time, steadily wearing it down until the mountain was gone. He would not do it with brute strength but with patience and persistent hard work, just as he was dealing with her doubts.

A fine mist caressed her face, a soft sensation that would refresh all it touched. Jarrod's concern and kindness were beginning to have a renewing effect on Jennifer's heart in much the same way.

The mist turned to showers and the showers to chilling torrents of early winter rains over the next few days. All the remaining stubborn foliage had been forced from the branches of most of the trees, leaving the countryside bleak after the abundant beauty of the past few weeks.

Jennifer took a deep breath and sighed as she strolled across the deserted mill yard. Working day shift on the weekends was a pleasant break from her normal routine. The damp earth and cut wood created an aromatic perfume that seemed to soothe away all troubles and unpleasantness. The warm sunshine had finally decided to reappear and was drying up the last remnants of the storms.

The day had gone so well that Jennifer was not even upset when she discovered someone had left the most remote of the perimeter gates open. The wide expanse of ground to the gate was a habitual mire of mud, sawdust, and water, making crossing it difficult.

Reluctantly, she began the tedious trek, carefully testing the surface of the ground under her feet before proceeding, one step at a time, across the boggy area. Her luck was holding nicely as she reached the halfway point. Only one hundred yards to go!

The hardened surface had dried sufficiently to sustain her weight. Then, suddenly the thin crust gave way, sucking her into the mire up to the calves of her legs. Each attempt she made to release her entrapped appendages only succeeded in sucking her deeper into the ooze.

Out of the corner of her eye, Jennifer caught sight of a moving object. As she turned in the direction of the movement, she saw Jarrod astride the beautiful stallion she had seen in the corral at the house. He was carefully and painstakingly coaxing the horse through the mud in her direction. Within a matter of minutes, the horse and rider stood within reach of the stranded woman.

"Don't you think you're a little old to be playing in the mud?" His voice sounded teasing, yet his face remained stern.

"No jokes! Just get me out of here!" Jennifer demanded.

"Doesn't look like you're in much of a position to be making demands to me. Come on, Lumberjack; let's go see if we can find a more appreciative damsel in distress somewhere."

"Jarrod, don't you dare leave me here like this."

"Why not? At least I'd know where you were and that you couldn't get into any more trouble."

"Jarrod, please."

"Well, Lumberjack, what do you think? Maybe we could help just a little." Jarrod bent over to pat the horse's neck, as if he was talking only to the animal.

"Jarrod! Come on! I'd get on my knees and beg, but I'm afraid I might get sucked under." Jennifer half pleaded and half returned his teasing.

"Well, I guess that's close enough to begging." Jarrod smiled as he reached down to pull her onto the saddle with him. But as he succeeded in securing her release from the clutches of the mud hole, a shoe slipped from her foot and was quickly swallowed by the quagmire. Jennifer was swung effortlessly across the saddle in front of Jarrod, her shoulder resting on his broad chest, his arms forming a protective circle around her.

"Will you ever learn to stay out of trouble?"

"The only time I get into trouble is when you're around. Maybe you're just bad luck," she snapped, angry at herself for not anticipating the dangers of this area and for losing the only pair of work shoes she owned.

"What in the world were you doing out here, anyway?"

"The back gate was open, so I was going to close it."

"Why didn't you just call me and ask me to come down and close it for you?"

Jennifer was silent at the simplicity of his statement.

A frown crossed Jarrod's brows as he waited for her answer.

"I didn't think of it," Jennifer mumbled in a weak voice.

"I thought that's what you're being paid to do," Jarrod scolded as he wiped a smudge of mud from her face.

"I'm sorry, I'm not perfect like some people seem to be," Jennifer retorted.

"Ouch! Lumberjack, maybe we should just leave her where we found her." Jarrod remarked as he playfully pretended to throw her back into the sea of mud. Jennifer grabbed his neck with all her strength, fearing he might just carry through with the threat. The sudden movement of both riders caused the already nervous horse to rear up, dumping both passengers unceremoniously back into the miry bog.

"Now see what you've done." Jarrod's tone was more of disgust than anger.

The sight of the normally impeccable Jarrod Drake sitting in a sea of mud erased any anger Jennifer had been harboring. Laughter began to bubble from her throat until she could no longer contain herself. She laughed at the two of them until tears ran down her cheeks, leaving small streaks in the mud. Jarrod's own displeasure also disappeared as he, too, became aware of the comedy in their situation. With a grin, he offered a muddy hand as they assisted each other to the perimeter of the mud puddle.

"It's going to be fun trying to drive home with this stuff all over me," Jennifer remarked, the complexity of the situation beginning to dawn on her. She had no chance of recovering her lost shoe; her legs and entire backside were now encased in the mud that would shortly begin to harden if it were not removed soon.

"Come on," Jarrod responded abruptly after he too had considered all the alternatives. He swept Jennifer into his arms, holding her close to his masculine chest. Then he picked up the reins of the horse and walked toward his house.

"Why don't we ride?" Jennifer asked as she contentedly wrapped her arms around his neck, seeing no need to waste the transportation.

"Are you complaining?" Jarrod glanced down at her as he tightened his hold.

"No, I was just curious," Jennifer replied, laying her head on his shoulder.

"Well, if you really want to know, I don't want to be up half the night cleaning mud off Lumberjack and the saddle. Cleaning off what's on him now is going to take long enough."

The half-mile trek up the gentle incline of the hill was accomplished in a short time, and Jennifer was amazed at how easily Jarrod had managed the climb with her added weight.

Jarrod let her slide from his arms onto the solid ground near the corral gate as he began to tie the horse to the wooden fence. After completing this task, he again took Jennifer in his arms and carried her up the steps onto the porch area surrounding the house. When he reached a smooth surface on the walk, he released her from his hold.

"There's a shower, first door on your left when you go in. Just leave your muddy clothes in the hall, and we'll wash them when you're finished. You should find towels and a robe in there, too." Not waiting for any argument or excuses, Jarrod turned and descended the stairs. "Take your time. I'm going to clean up Lumberjack."

Jennifer was relieved to find everything just as he had said. As she removed her soiled garments, she was careful not to make yet another mess on the bathroom floor. Once the clothes were deposited in the hallway, she stepped into the shower and let the hot, stinging spray remove the caking mud from her hair and body. She was only now beginning to realize how tense she had been until she felt the water begin to relax her taunt muscles. Jennifer had no idea how long she had allowed the soothing cascade of water, but a sudden knocking on the bathroom door brought her back to reality.

"I hope you saved some hot water for me," Jarrod's voice teased.

Jennifer turned off the water immediately, suddenly aware she had been in the shower a very long time.

"I'm finished," she called back, grabbing a towel through the cloud of steam that filled the room. She dried herself quickly and wrapped another towel turban style around her damp hair. The robe Jarrod had mentioned was hanging on the back of the door. The dark brown velour material had absorbed some of the steam filling the small room, causing it to cling to Jennifer's body as she slipped into the extra-large garment. The coolness of the fabric against her warmed body sent shivers over her skin. A faint hint of rich masculine cologne brought a new sense of awareness to the figure standing half-hidden in the mist of the room. As she opened the door, clouds of steam rolled out into the hallway.

"Now I know you used all the hot water," Jarrod complained half-seriously as he fanned his arms to dispense the vapor that surrounded them both. A smile of approval brightened the tanned face as his gaze ran from her towel-wrapped head to the tips of her toes barely visible under the long robe.

Jarrod had discarded his own muddy clothes and added them to Jennifer's, replacing them with a pair of aged sport shorts. The sight of the virile breadth of his shirtless torso shot tingles through Jennifer, adding deeper hues to the already bright pinks of her skin.

Jarrod placed his hands on her shoulders and turned her in the direction of the living room. "You'd better go sit by the fire before you catch a cold." He spoke in a fatherly tone that irritated Jennifer.

The fire blazed with an intensity that brightened the entire room as the early winter's darkness enveloped the house and its occupants in a cocoon of isolation.

"I've already called the oncoming guards and told them where you are so they won't start looking for you around the mill. I also called your mother and explained the situation to her so she won't worry about your being late." She was glad he had been so thoughtful because she had neglected to think of anyone else but the two of them.

"You have been busy. Did you get Lumberjack cleaned up?" Jennifer asked as she gazed into the dancing flames.

"Yes, and even had time to get the fire started, just for you. Here, drink this, it'll make you feel better," he said, handing her a steaming cup of hot chocolate with a generous helping of whipped cream floating on top. The cup felt warm as she gripped it and took a hesitant sip of the scalding liquid.

"Now you just stay here and get warm. I'll be back soon; I should have some hot water by now." His smile was pleasant as he bounded up the stairs and disappeared into the master bedroom. The parting look he had given her warmed her more than either the chocolate or the blazing fire could.

The warmth of the fire soon replaced the cool dampness of the robe. Jennifer moved from her seat on the hearth to the soft comfort of the carpet and pillows on the floor. The combination of the warmth and peacefulness of her surroundings drew her into the relaxing, comforting world of sleep.

Her lips responded naturally to the gentle persuasion of the firm mouth that touched and teased. A sigh slipped softly from her throat; *dreams could be so real.* She smiled as she savored the exquisite feel of the masculine hand that cradled her cheek ever so lightly.

"I warned you about sleeping like that." The male voice was husky as he whispered close to her ear.

Jennifer opened her eyes. Jarrod was lying on his side next to her. Shimmering lights seemed to be dancing around his glistening ebony head. The intoxicating fragrances of soap and cologne only heightened her awareness of this prime example of manhood lying so close to her now.

Jarrod propped himself up on one elbow and ran the fingers of his free hand along her cheek. His happy and contented expression brought a glow of joy to her face, as did the sparkle of pleasure she saw reflected in his eyes.

"I thought I was dreaming," Jennifer confessed.

"I'm afraid you'll just have to put up with me until your dream man comes along."

Jennifer breathed an exaggerated sigh. "I guess we can't have everything."

"Maybe we should see if dreams really do come true." Drawing her into his arms, Jarrod kissed the corners of her lips, only brushing their fullness until she felt she could stand no more anticipation. Gently, tenderly, as if he were implanting each touch to memory, he at last kissed her lips.

Jennifer eagerly returned his kisses with more passion than she had ever expressed for anyone. Jarrod was everything she'd ever wanted.

Suddenly Jennifer pulled away. Was he everything she'd dreamed of, or did he *have* everything she wanted—peace with himself and God? She felt her throat constrict as the doubts flooded her mind. Was she doing the same thing again her father had accused her of doing? Was she trying to find her peace and happiness through someone else?

Jarrod released his hold and saw the fears and doubts she was trying to hide. He stroked the silky strands of hair. He could see the remembered pain of losing her dad she had loved so much. She was afraid of loving and losing again. She was afraid of sharing her feelings and dreams with someone else. But most of all, she was afraid of something else, something that overshadowed everything. That was the one fear he could not grasp, not until she chose to share it with him.

He pulled her close one last time. Her mistakes were in the past. Now it was time for the healing to begin, if only she would accept what was being offered to her. But no matter how much Jarrod wanted to help, this was one journey she would have to take on her own.

"I think it's time we got you home, young lady." Jarrod's voice seemed distant as if someone else were speaking the words.

As he stood he pulled Jennifer up with him. Obeying his unspoken command, Jennifer walked in a silent daze to the bathroom and changed back into her now clean and dry uniform and socks. As usual, Jarrod had taken care of everything. She saw no need to wear only one shoe, so she returned to the living room in her stocking feet. Jarrod stood with his back to her, facing the fireplace as she entered the room unobserved.

"Oh, God, please help me!" Jarrod suddenly exclaimed as his fist hit against the stone wall in front of him with such force that Jennifer jumped in surprise. Never had she seen so much confusion on Jarrod's face as the moment he turned from the fireplace and saw her standing just a few feet behind him.

The silence seemed to stretch for hours before Jarrod spoke. "Are you ready?"

"Yes." Her voice now sounded like someone else speaking.

"I'll have one of my men bring your car to your house tomorrow," he said, taking her elbow and walking briskly toward the front door.

Both were absorbed in their own thoughts as they walked across the deck and down the front steps. Just as Jennifer started to step onto the cold bare ground of the driveway in her stocking feet, Jarrod swept her into his arms and carried her to the company truck. Still holding her close to his chest, he opened the door and sat her on the seat.

As they entered the main road, a county sheriff's patrol car stopped and flashed his lights.

"Wonder what he wants?" Jennifer questioned as the unit turned around and pulled up beside Jarrod's side of the vehicle.

"Mr. Drake, I've been looking for you. Heard you called the office and wanted to talk to me."

"I have to take Miss Kent home now; why don't you meet me at my office in about half an hour?"

"Fine. See you then."

"Is there something wrong?" Jennifer questioned as soon as the deputy was out of hearing range.

"I'm not sure yet. I'll let you know as soon as I can."

The short drive to the Kent home seemed to take forever. Jarrod was deep in thought and said nothing the whole trip, and Jennifer felt only more confusion.

Jarrod repeated the previous scene when they reached the house, lifting her from the seat and cradling her in his arms until they reached the front door of the house.

"Jennifer ..."

"Goodnight, Jarrod." Jennifer cut him short.

He bent to kiss her, but she avoided his lips. He settled instead for her forehead and then pushed open the front door. He held her in his arms a few seconds longer before sitting her down just inside the living room. Then he turned and walked back into the night.

Jennifer closed the door behind him and listened to the sound of the truck as it drove away until it also disappeared into the blackness of the night. Thankful her mother was sound asleep at this late hour, she climbed the flight of stairs that led to her cold, dark, and empty room.

CHAPTER

....

7

....

Rumors had spread rapidly around the mill concerning the late-night visit of the deputy sheriff. Numerous speculations were the main topic of discussion for the next couple of day.

Jarrod had made no attempt to contact Jennifer, and she only caught brief glimpses of him at a distance. A check of the security logs told her he had remained in his office long after the deputy had departed. Even after the office lights were turned off, his truck remained parked on the grounds until the wee hours of the morning.

Even at a distance, Jennifer was able to sense Jarrod was struggling with an immense burden. She longed to be able to go to him and offer some type of comfort, but what could she do? A noise somewhere between a laugh and a cry escaped her throat.

"You can't even help yourself!" she said to the stillness around her.

All during her shift, Jennifer couldn't shake the feeling that though she couldn't see him, Jarrod was not far away.

The country lanes were deserted as she started home after work at midnight. A thick covering of clouds had blocked out the stars, and even the moon only occasionally broke through to lessen the inky blackness that had settled onto the valley floor.

A slight shiver ran up Jennifer's arms as she drove down the silent main street. It had been a long time since she had felt the need to be with other people, to have those around her who really cared how she felt and loved her even when she made mistakes.

Blinking to hold back the trickle of tears that were forming in her beautiful eyes, Jennifer quietly realized that what she wanted was to be loved, but more specifically, she wanted Jarrod's love. The thought filled her heart to overflowing. Jarrod was everything she had ever dreamed of, and his quiet strength gave her the courage to once again search for the answers to the questions Ezra had forced her to ask herself. Jarrod had accepted her doubts without condemning and preaching to her, as some had done when she first began to question beliefs she had always accepted as fact.

He hadn't tried to push Scriptures or doctrine down her throat. He had merely told her about the principles he believed in and shared sources that had helped him. He had allowed her the freedom to think about the information he had chosen to share with her without expecting any response.

A serene smile softened her features as she pulled into the driveway of her childhood home. Ezra would have approved of Jarrod. In many ways, there were very much alike. Both shared an unshakable faith and trust in an almighty God. Both were men others looked up to; even if they didn't always agree, both were still respected for standing by their convictions.

This new feeling was too much for Jennifer to keep to herself as she mischievously shut the back door harder than necessary.

"Jennifer, is that you?" Mrs. Kent called from upstairs.

"Yes, Mom, did I wake you?"

"No, but if I had been that door would have."

"Good!" Jennifer stood in the door of the bedroom, a broad smile brightening her face. "Since you aren't asleep, want to talk?"

Mrs. Kent met her daughter's happy smile with one of her own. "You know I'm always ready to talk with you, dear." At the same time she reached for the light beside her bed, and sitting up against the pillows, she patted the edge of the mattress.

Jennifer sat cross-legged across from her mother and studied the woman before her. The years had been good to Mrs. Kent, but Jennifer couldn't remember when she had grown so much older. She wasn't sure when the gray had stolen away the luscious brown locks her dad had loved so much or when the wrinkles had begun to replace the soft, smooth, youthful skin she had remembered. This woman had given her life, love, and guidance without ever having expressed regret or disappointment in the person she had helped produce.

Jennifer swallowed the lump in her throat before she spoke. "Mom, I'm sorry for this morning. I didn't mean to be so sharp or to hurt you in any way."

"I know, dear, and I didn't mean to pry. But I know how much you're hurting, and I only wanted to help in some way. If there were any way I could take some of your pain upon myself and spare you I would, but honey, you have to work through this yourself. I'd just hoped that talking about whatever's troubling you might help."

"I know. Jarrod ... Jarrod's been ... trying to help, too."

"You love him, don't you, dear?"

"How did you know?" Jennifer was surprised at her mother's observation, since she had only recently realized the truth.

"I've seen the sparkle in your eyes whenever he's around and the change in you over the past few weeks."

"But Mom, I'm so scared."

"Child, of what? You must know how he feels about you."

"No, I don't know."

"Jennifer, he may not have said so in words, but I know that Jarrod cares very deeply for you. And he's wonderful man. He and your father really got along well. I think if we had not been blessed with a daughter, your dad would have wanted a son like Jarrod."

"They're a lot alike, you know." Jennifer's voice was a husky whisper as she spoke of feelings so near her heart.

"Yes, at times when Jarrod is sitting in your father's favorite chair, I can almost see or hear Ezra."

"He's only been here that day we went to Eureka." Jennifer was puzzled by her mother's statement.

"Oh, no, dear, after your father died, Jarrod helped me more than anyone else. He often came by to see if I needed any work done. Then when his own dad died so suddenly, I think he just wanted company. It's only been since you've been home that he hasn't been coming around, but he still calls to make sure nothing needs fixing."

"He never once mentioned any of this."

"Jarrod's not one that goes around bragging about the things he's done. If he sees something that needs doing, he simply does it."

"Why didn't he know me when I went to work at the mill then?"

"Jennifer, when was the last time you had a picture taken of yourself? Your graduation picture, right? And young lady, you've changed quite a bit since then." The teasing smiled seemed to wipe away the years as they both remembered the skinny teenager who had been ready to take on the whole world.

"I don't remember seeing him at the funeral."

"Jarrod was out of town when your father went to be with the Lord, but he came back as soon as he could. Jennifer, why didn't ... never mind, I don't want to pry."

"Why didn't I stay around after the funeral?" Jennifer finished her mother's question. The sadness that flickered across Mrs. Kent's face was reflected in Jennifer's own solemn face. "I couldn't stand the thought of coming back here, knowing that Dad would never be coming home again. Mom, I needed to talk to him, and now I can't."

"Honey, don't you think he'll know when you've found the answers to your questions?"

"Mom, at one time everything was so simple and now ..."

"Jennifer, life has never been simple; you just didn't know that life was more than your own little world. I'm afraid that's what happens when you grow up."

Jennifer laughed softly as Mrs. Kent tried in vain to stifle a yawn. "I think it's past someone's bedtime."

"I think you're right. Jennifer, everything will work out for the best between you and Jarrod."

"I don't know."

"Do you have a problem you haven't told me about?"

"I guess I'm just scared."

"Of what?"

"Of loving him and then ..."

"Losing him? Jennifer, God doesn't give us someone to share our lives with without having some special reason, and that reason and the wonderful times you'll have shared together will make the pain bearable until you're together again in heaven."

"Mom, what do you think ... never mind." Jennifer left her question unasked as she rose from the bed and started toward the door.

"Why God brought your father and me together?"

Jennifer stopped and turned around; a brief nod was her only response.

"You." Mrs. Kent reached for the light and plunged the room into darkness.

"Good night, Mom. I love you." Jennifer closed the door to her mother's room and walked in the shadowy darkness of the hall to her former bedroom.

For a long time sleep eluded Jennifer as she watched the shadows playing across the floor of her room when the moon was able to escape the clouds trying to block out its light. She wanted desperately to help Jarrod with whatever was troubling him, but only Jarrod and the Lord ... Jennifer sat up in her bed. She had actually thought about the Lord and felt no doubt that He did exist. He did exist—if not for her, He certainly did for Jarrod and would help him; of that she was sure.

Sometime during the night, the overcast skies turned stormy as rain drenched the valley unmercifully and lighting and thunder clashed to disturb the peace of the tiny mountain hamlet.

Jennifer tossed and turned with the storm, never quite waking but feeling the fury of the storm that lashed just outside her window.

Uncertainty clouded Jennifer's heart as she awoke to a dark and dreary day. She felt tired and as restless as the wind that violently whipped the trees outside her window.

"Good morning, dear. Didn't you sleep well?" Mrs. Kent handed her daughter a cup of hot coffee.

Jennifer sighed as she accepted the mug and sat down at the kitchen table. "I felt fine when I went to bed, but I sure didn't sleep well."

"Is something still troubling you? I thought you had settled everything last night."

"I don't know what's wrong. I just know something's bothering Jarrod, and I can't help."

"Honey, have you prayed about it?"

Jennifer stared into the rich brown liquid in front of her and remained quiet.

Patting her daughter's hand as she rose, Mrs. Kent continued, "I'll do some praying for both of you, dear."

"Thanks."

The storm continued to cast its fury across the valley floor for the rest of the day. Wind and lightning played havoc with lines throughout the valley, periodically interrupting power. The radio reported minor flooding along the creek banks, and rock and mud slides kept cleanup crews busy along the state highways.

"You'd better dress warm tonight, Jennifer." Mrs. Kent stood looking out the picture window of the living room as she spoke.

"I plan to stay inside as much as possible."

"Please be careful. It's really nasty out there."

Jennifer smiled at her mother's concern as she continued putting the final touches on her uniform. The yellow rain slicker was much too long and touched the tops of her rain boots, but it was the best she could do with the small selection of sizes the security company had sent for her to distribute among her workers.

The drive to the mill was impeded by the intensity of the downpour, with visibility reduced to less than half a block at times. Jennifer shuddered as a blast of wind violently buffeted her compact car. This was going to be one miserable evening, even if she did manage to stay indoors most of the time.

The only bright spot of the day came when she spotted Jarrod's pickup parked outside the main office building. Maybe she'd be able to find out what was troubling him.

"Hi, Andrea," Jennifer said as cheerfully as she could manage, shaking the excess water off her raincoat and trying not to get the office floor any wetter than it already was.

"Hi, yourself. I certainly don't envy you tonight. But I might give you a thought or two as Dan and I are curled up in front of the fireplace." Andrea grinned mischievously as she gathered her belongings and straightened her desk.

"Andrea, did you get those reports I ask for yet?" Jarrod called from his office.

"Yes, sir, they're on the corner of your desk," Andrea replied patiently. "He's seen better days too," she commented so that only Jennifer could hear.

"Andrea, when Miss Kent ..." Jarrod stopped short as he came out of his office and noticed the two ladies standing next to his secretary's desk. "Miss Kent, I'd like to speak to you in my office if you have the time."

"Now is fine with me," Jennifer said, feeling warm and sunny despite the early winter squall releasing its wrath unmercifully upon everything in its path just outside the door.

Jarrod barely looked at Jennifer as he waited for her to enter his office. He motioned for her to take one of the seats in front of his desk instead of her usual place on the sofa and closed the door to his office.

Silently obliging him, Jennifer was surprised at the clutter of handwritten notes, computer printouts, and reports that now lay in a confused mess on his normally well-organized desk.

Jennifer watched as he settled himself into his chair and took in a deep breath before he bent over to pick up a stack of papers and deposited them unceremoniously on the bookshelf beside his desk. Deep lines of fatigue were etched around the corners of his eyes. The normal sparkling luster of his dark eyes had been replaced by a dullness that seemed to be a mixture of sadness, anger, and confusion. Shock bolted through her heart at how in the space of only a few days he seemed to have aged beyond his thirty-odd years. His shoulders drooped, as if he carried the weight of the world on them.

"Jennifer," Jarrod's voice was low as he began to speak, "has anything unusual happened here at the mill that you have failed to mention in any of your reports?"

A frown of confusion crossed her face as she replied to his question. "Jarrod, I've always reported anything that's happened here, no matter how minor, and so have the other guards as far as I know. Why? Is something wrong?"

"In the last three weeks, we have had more than two flatbeds of lumber disappear off the yard, and yet I've found nothing in any of your reports to indicate anything unusual has happened. No after-hours trucks, no pickups on the yard, nothing. How do you account for that?"

As the implications of Jarrod's statement began to sink in, Jennifer felt the shock strike her almost physically. "I haven't seen anything unusual. Maybe it's just some kind of bookkeeping error or something."

"Don't you think I want to believe that?" Jarrod struck his fist against the desktop before he stood abruptly and walked toward the glass wall behind his desk, his back toward the stunned woman he had come to care for so deeply. At this moment, the doubts and confusion that clouded his heart and mind prevented him from facing her directly with the questions that demanded answers.

"Jennifer," his voice was thick with emotion as he spoke, still unable to turn and face her directly, afraid of what she might unwillingly tell him, "do you know anything about these thefts?"

"What!" Jennifer sprang to her feet, unprepared for the accusations his simple question implied. "Jarrod, how could you think I would have anything to do with any of this?"

"What do you expect me to think? We've never had anything like this happen before. The only way anyone could pull off something as large as this is to have someone on the security force helping them."

"So you think I'm involved in some way. Jarrod, how could you after ..." Her voice trailed off, and she could no longer see anything but a blur as a veil of tears began to slide down her cheeks.

"After what? A few kisses! You wouldn't be the first woman in history to try and trick a man, now would you?" Jarrod felt a sickening feeling deep in his gut as he watched the emotions that played across Jennifer's face. He didn't like this one bit. Hadn't he told the Sheriff's Department from the beginning there had to be another way? But they had insisted that Jennifer was the one person who had the key to this whole operation.

"If you think I'm involved with this, why don't you just have me arrested and get it all over with!" Her words were spit out with a mixture of anger, hurt, and betrayal.

Jarrod ached to take her in his arms and assure her that everything would be all right—that together they would find out who was behind the thefts.

Jennifer turned to leave the suffocating confines of Jarrod's office, upsetting the chair in her hasty flight for freedom. Blinded by her own rage, she stumbled over the overturned piece of furniture and would have fallen to the floor if a pair of strong hands had not caught her in mid-air.

"Get your hands off me!" Jennifer screamed as she fought to break loose from Jarrod's hold. His touch seemed to burn her flesh almost as painfully as his words had seared her tender heart, now shattered and aching within her breast.

"Jennifer, listen to me, please."

"Let me go! Haven't you said enough?"

Jarrod held her for only the briefest of moments before he reluctantly let her go and watched as she fled from his office.

Jarrod watched as raindrops slid silently down the glass wall of his office. He could see Jennifer's retreating figure running across the mill yard. For the second time he was watching her depart from his life, only this time the void he felt was much too deep to heal without leaving scars. She would always be a part of him, no matter what the future held.

"Dear God, please give me strength and understanding to see me through whatever You have in store, because there is no way to make it through this without You. Once again I feel like I'm on the beach and I see only one set of footprints." Jarrod felt a tear slide down his cheek, but he just let it trickle down the bristled stubble that had accumulated on his face over the last couple of days. Still he continued to watch Jennifer until she disappeared around the corner of the mill's main building.

Jennifer hadn't noticed that the winter storm had subsided as an even more violent one now raged within her heart. A gust of wind blew across the yard and chilled her flesh just as Jarrod's words had chilled her heart.

It seemed like hours she had walked in a daze around the yard until she found herself standing between the rows of logs in the deck area. They offered both solitude and protection from the chilling winds and a chance for her senses to recover from their numbed state.

As she stood and watched a pair of ground squirrels scurry to and from their newly acquired home among the stacks of logs, she felt her own position drawn into perspective. The squirrels were busily storing up supplies for the long winter that lay ahead, falsely feeling they would be secure, warm, and happy when the dead of winter was upon them. Little did they know all their work would be in vain, because someday Mr. Jarrod Drake's giant machinery would come and tear apart their shelter with its huge prongs. Then what would they have? Nothing at all, thanks to Mr. Drake.

At least now Jennifer knew exactly where she stood. He really thought she would try to steal from him. Shaking her head in disbelief, she walked alongside the two-story-high stacks of uncut logs that served as a buffer from all the hustle and bustle of the mill. He had actually had the nerve to accuse her of trying to trick him into thinking she cared for him; hadn't he done the same thing to her? She resolved to take care of that little problem. The shelter she would build around her heart would serve her well in protecting her from any future attacks from Mr. Drake. She would see to that—and the sooner the better.

"I'll show him!" Jennifer struck a blow to the end of a protruding log as she spoke and immediately regretted her actions as a sharp pain traveled with lightning speed up her arm. Gripping her smarting hand, she watched with disbelief as a thick, dark red substance oozed between her fingers. Wiping the liquid away from the wound, she was surprised to find her skin was unbroken. The end of the log had far too much of this substance to have come from her hand. Jennifer began a gradual check of the area and noted several large puddles of the bloodlike matter beneath several of the logs along the deck.

"It's called bleeding sap." Jarrod's voice startled Jennifer as she examined her new find. He hesitated, as if giving Jennifer a chance to decide whether she wanted him to remain or leave before he continued. "It's common in all trees except cedar and redwood. After they're cut, the heat brings the sap out." Jarrod almost reverently touched a trail of the scarlet liquid. "Sometimes I feel it's the way wood expresses its sorrow for having been the means by which our Lord was put to death."

"How dare you talk to me about God and Jesus after what you just accused me of? You can trust a God you've never seen, but you can't believe a word I say. Oh, but then I'm just a human, and a woman at that, who is not above being deceitful to get what she wants. Now you listen to me, Jarrod Drake, I may be a lot of things, but I'm not a liar or a thief, and don't you forget it."

"Jennifer, what do you expect me to do? Just pretend that nothing's happening because you might be involved? I can't just bury my head. Jennifer, if there's anything you can tell me, please, for both our sakes, tell me."

"Come on, Jarrod, you don't have to pretend you care anymore, I know better; your heart is as cold and hard as that wood."

"You have a lot to learn about wood, Miss Kent. It is not always hard, and it certainly isn't cold, especially when it's ignited by a highly combustible source. Besides you have pointed out it can bleed when it's cut or damaged. Things are not always as they seem."

"You're certainly right about that, Mr. Drake, especially so-called Christians."

Jennifer turned and walked away. As she headed toward the mill, she hoped to find some protection from further contact from Jarrod for the still fragile shell she was determined to build around her bruised and aching heart.

CHAPTER

....

8

....

After the events of the past week, each long day passed into another equally dreary one without much hope of any changes in the future.

Winter fogs began to settle onto the valley floor, creating an eerie, dreamlike atmosphere shrouding the mill and yard. Objects were easily concealed from view, even when they were relatively close by. The bleak wind shifted the dense mist, continually changing the general appearance of the area.

The environment matched Jennifer's mood perfectly—the dull numbness she felt in her heart, the need to seek quiet solitude for a short while, the desire to blend inconspicuously into her surroundings. She shed no more tears; she had shed too many already. She felt no agonizing pain or remorse, only a cold, empty void that made everything appear meaningless and unimportant.

A faint whiff of burning oil caught her attention, disappearing as quickly as it had appeared. Jennifer dismissed any cause for alarm, attributing the odor to a worker using one of the pieces of heavy equipment.

Her footsteps echoed loudly in the huge, vacant metal building, adding to her feelings of insignificance and isolation. After indifferently completing her check of the area, Jennifer pulled the pile collar of her uniform jacket up around her neck and ears in anticipation of the chilling blast of the wind and damp fog awaiting her outside the protective door. After stuffing a gloved hand deep into her pocket, she pushed open the metal door and braced herself. Instead of biting cold, a flash of hot black smoke stung her eyes and filled her lungs, robbing them of fresh air.

Quickly closing the door, Jennifer felt her way toward the foreman's office, yelling for assistance between coughing spasms to clear her lungs. Her eyes, though still burning and watery, had cleared enough by the time she reached the telephone to enable her to dial the local fire department. As soon as this was done, Jarrod should be notified next.

Jennifer held her breath as she dialed the number and waited for the call to go through. Her apprehension turned to agitation with each successive unanswered ring. Convinced no one was home, she started to replace the receiver but caught a distant voice before she was able to hang up.

"Jarrod!"

"Yes."

His voice sounded hollow and weary, or maybe it was only her imagination. "The oil shed is burning! The fire department's on its way, but I thought you'd want to be here."

"Is anything else in danger?" More life was beginning to flow into his previously vacant tone of speech.

Jennifer could not help but admire the calm and practicality Jarrod displayed in the midst of the pandemonium that was making her heart pound wildly against her breast.

"So far everything else is okay. The oil shed probably won't be saved and I see lots of smoke, but that's about it."

"Did someone unlock the gates for the fire trucks?"

"Yes, I gave my key to Earle."

"Good. I knew I could count on you not to lose your head. I'll be right down." The click at the other end of the line ended the conversation.

Somehow his confidence in her abilities and subsequent compliment did not bring the thrill it would have at another time. She was only doing what he had expected from her all along: a job well done. Now it was too late to make any difference, she thought sadly as she replaced the receiver into its cradle.

Millworkers had already manned the company's fire hoses by the time Jennifer arrived from the foreman's office. The crackling, hissing sounds emanating from the burning building suggested the flames were laughing at the men's feeble attempts to control them.

Rivers of burning oil began to flood the ground surrounding the building, spreading the inferno of potential devastation across everything in its path.

"Get that water off there and start watering down the walls of the mill!" The sharp command brought everyone to an abrupt halt as Jarrod slammed the door of his truck. Grimly, he strode to the head of the hose line and took control of the nozzle, directing it away from the fire and onto the metal walls of the mill facing the burning building.

Vapors of steam hissed from the sides of the building as torrents of cold water bombarded the heated metal to cool it.

The flashing red lights of the responding fire trucks rolled through the gates and onto the yard. The wail of their sirens, crackling radios, shouts of commands, and roar of the fire all combined to create a scene of rapid-fire confusion. Cans inside the burning building were beginning to explode with a fair amount of regularity. The noise level had risen sharply within a matter of minutes, making it extremely difficult to hear even a person standing nearby.

The building was totally engulfed in flames as the fire trucks came to a halt a safe distance from their objective. The most that could be accomplished would be to contain the fire at its present location and prevent any heat damage to any of the other nearby buildings.

A foam truck was positioned about one hundred yards from the inferno and began to spray its thick, steady stream of chemical suppressant material onto the blaze. A dense carpet of foam slowly began to accumulate around the remains of the shed. Within a few minutes, the flames were completely smothered by the creamy white blanket. The once-raging scene was extinguished without so much as a final rebellious flare up, only quiet submission.

Jennifer stood at the edge of the small group watching the activities. She felt a sense of amazement and excitement as the level of battle increased. Occasionally she caught glimpses of Jarrod in conference with the fire chief or on some errand. He seemed to be everywhere but never in the way or interfering with the efforts of the firefighters.

News of the fire had spread rapidly around the small community. Small crowds of spectators were beginning to form along the roads leading to the mill, and some even wandered onto the mill property. Workers and security alike had their hands full trying to keep equipment moving in an orderly manner. Local sheriff's deputies were called out to help with the quickly growing crowd.

Some of the clean-up operations had begun when Jarrod called for Jennifer to join the small group of people surrounding him.

"Do you know who discovered the fire?"

"I guess I did." Jennifer reported to the circle of men looking to her for answers to their unasked questions. "When I started to come out of the mill after I finished my rounds, the smoke nearly took my breath away."

"Do you know who was oiling the machinery tonight?" Jarrod asked, trying to determine who would be most likely to have been going in and out of the building most of the evening.

"I'm not sure, but I think Steve was. Do you want me to get him for you?" Jennifer asked, trying to be as helpful as she could since she knew little about the origin of the fire.

"Go ahead. Tell him we'll be here going through the debris." Jarrod dismissed her from the group, and Jennifer eagerly hurried to accomplish her assigned task.

It didn't take long to find the worker because most of the men were huddled together discussing the evening's events well out of sight of their boss. Jennifer relayed her message and then went on to the mill office to report the fire to Lieutenant Edwards. After several tries, she finally succeeded in reaching his answering service but was told he was not in at the present time and they had no idea where he was or how he could be reached. Jennifer briefly told them what had occurred and that she would try to reach her boss sometime the following day.

The small groups of men that Jennifer had left were standing next to the remains of the destroyed building when she returned after completing her tasks. A fine mist of water was being sprayed onto the gooey white mass to dissipate it and reveal any secrets that might be concealed beneath.

Jennifer watched in transfixed fascination as the men slowly shifted through the ashes and burned and bent cans. One of the investigators picked up a badly deformed metal can and examined it closely before showing it to the others in attendance.

"Steve, did you put this can in the shed?" Jarrod's question reflected his own growing concern as to the cause of the fire.

"No, sir, and I don't remember seeing it here when I made my last pickup before the fire."

"I hate to say this, Mr. Drake, but it really looks like this may be arson," the chief of the fire department reported to those standing by.

"But why?" Steve questioned. "Nothing of value was in here except oil for the machinery. We keep most of the fuel at the garage. This building wasn't close enough to the mill to really endanger it. This really doesn't make much sense."

"Maybe the shed wasn't the object of whoever set it on fire? Maybe this was just some kind of distraction." Jarrod thought over his statement, looking for some clue to the evening's events.

Before anyone had a chance to voice their own opinions, the local deputy joined the thoughtful group.

"The roads have all been cleared, Mr. Drake. But I left the back gate unlocked so the fire truck could get out."

"We don't have any equipment on any part of the yard except here," the chief informed the surprised officer.

"But I saw the lights of a big truck over behind the lumber near the north side of the yard," insisted the confused officer.

"That gate wasn't opened when I came down right after the fire was reported," Jarrod said. "Maybe we'll soon find out just why we had our fire." Jarrod shouted orders to block all exits with the company equipment as he ran for his truck.

"Where do you think you're going?" Jarrod demanded as Jennifer caught up with him and started to climb into the truck.

"With you. After all, security is part of my job here, remember!" Jennifer reminded him as she finished climbing into the truck and waited for him to either close the door or forcibly haul her out of the vehicle. For a few seconds it seemed as if he was seriously considering doing just that.

"You just stay out of the way if anything happens," Jarrod hissed through clenched teeth as he slammed the door and started the truck with a sudden jerk.

Jennifer bit the inside of her lip to keep a triumphant smile from penetrating her determined façade.

Neither occupant said a word during the short drive to the area where an intruder might be waiting. Jarrod turned off the engine and let the truck coast silently behind the protective cover of one of the lumber sheds. After they exited the vehicle, they stood quietly in the dark listening for any noise that might give them a clue as to what they were up against.

The sound of a diesel motor drifted through the fog. If the sounds were true and had not been distorted by the murky air, the persons they were searching for were just ahead.

Jarrod motioned to the deputy to circle around the building while he went in the opposite direction.

"Jennifer, you stay here in the truck with the radios. Get some help over here if you hear any trouble or we're not back soon." His whispered voice was strained with tension as he pushed Jennifer back toward the pickup.

"Jarrod ..." Jennifer started to speak but couldn't find the words to tell him how she felt. "Take care."

"I usually do." He smiled as he gently squeezed her arm and then disappeared into the fog.

Only the murmur of the equipment on the other side of the building broke the silence. Jennifer's heart pounded wildly against her chest with apprehension as each second passed.

Suddenly shouts and the clamor of a scuffle sent Jennifer running in the direction Jarrod had just taken. Rounding the corner of the protective barrier, two bodies engaged in a struggle bumped into her, sending all three toppling to the ground. A string of profanity issued from one of the combatants as the two men discovered what they had tripped over.

"Jennifer, get out of here!" Jarrod ordered as he ducked a fist intended for his jaw. The punch missed its target, but the dark-clad opponent lost his balance and fell headlong into Jarrod's midsection, sending both men sprawling onto the uneven surface of the hard ground.

The intruder scrambled to his feet and grabbed Jennifer around the neck with his forearm, cutting off her windpipe. "All right, Mr. High and Mighty, just stay right where you are and the little lady will be just fine."

Jennifer recognized her captor's voice the moment he spoke, and her anger overcame any thought of danger as she began to kick at his shins and scratch and bite the exposed skin on the arm around her chin. She managed to execute a sloppy shoulder throw and in the process set herself free.

The unidentified culprit landed in a spread eagle position right in front of Jarrod. As he started to rise, he attempted to sneak a punch at the overpowering form directly in front of his line of escape, but with the swiftness of a man half his size, Jarrod swung a jab to the midsection that knocked the man onto his back, clutching his stomach in pain.

Jarrod, rubbing his sore knuckles, walked over to the groaning man lying on the ground. Grabbing the man by the shoulder, he pulled him to a standing position. Even in the dim headlights of the idling forklift, Jennifer's recognition was confirmed.

"Glen!" She gasped. "How could you?"

A snarl crossed his lips as he cast a disgusted look in Jennifer's direction.

"Who are you working with?" Jarrod demanded through clenched teeth.

A smug laugh enhanced the evil appearance of the would-be thief. "You're so smart, you figure it out!"

Before Jarrod could continue questioning the suspect, the deputy sheriff wearily walked out of the mist and paused to catch his breath.

"Sorry, Mr. Drake, but the other one got away from me in the fog. Did this one tell you anything?"

"I'm afraid not, but at least they didn't get away with any lumber, and I noticed his hands smell like gasoline. It's my guess he started the oil shed fire as a diversion while he and his partner loaded the flatbed with lumber."

"It shouldn't be too hard to trace the truck and find his partner," the deputy sheriff reassured those present as he handcuffed his prisoner and began walking him back toward the patrol unit.

"I'm not going to take the fall for this. If you weren't so blind, maybe you'd know who else was in on this, or maybe you don't want to know. Ain't that right, Ms. Kent?" Glen shouted as he struggled against the deputy's attempts to put him in the back of the vehicle.

No one made a sound as the car drove off into the mist, but Jennifer could feel Jarrod's eyes focused on her back. She turned around to face the questions she knew he was thinking, whether or not they were spoken.

"You don't think I had anything to do with this, do you?"

Jarrod sighed as he ran his hand through his dark hair. "Jennifer, I honestly don't know what to believe anymore."

"Well, then maybe I should just quit and that would solve everything, wouldn't it?"

"And run away again? Jennifer, don't you think it's time to face up to your problems and resolve them? If you run away, everything will still be the same and someday you're going to run out of places to hide."

"What am I supposed to do? Everyone here thinks I'm involved in the thefts. No one believes me when I say I'm not, not even you. Just what am I supposed to do?"

"Prove that everybody's wrong. Help find out who is behind all this."

"Jarrod, be realistic. Even the police have no idea who's behind this. This is not some movie on TV where the crime gets solved in an hour and everyone's happy again."

"I didn't say anything like that. You're one smart lady, and who else would have more to gain by finding the thieves than you? Unless there's some reason you don't want to find out who else is involved?"

CHAPTER

9

"Hi, Jen! Where have you been keeping yourself lately? Haven't seen you in ages."

"I've been around, just busy." Jennifer toyed with the cord of the telephone as she tried to give a hint of believability to her words. She had made a special effort to try and avoid as many people as possible. Jarrod wouldn't say anything to anyone about what had happened—she was sure of that—but in a small town rumors have a way of spreading. No one had said a word to her, but she could see the unspoken accusations and insinuations in their eyes.

"Listen, I'm giving a little birthday party for Dan this Saturday night and wondered if you'd like to come." Andrea's voice was bright and carefree; Jennifer envied the happiness her friend had found.

"I don't know," Jennifer hedged, unable to come up with any excuses not to accept the invitation.

"Oh, come on, Jen. Please! A couple of the guys from the fire station have been asking about you. At least say you'll come for a little while."

"I'd like to, but I won't have a way out there. I'm taking my car into the garage on Friday, and they said it won't be out until sometime next week." This was partly true; her car was going in for repairs and wouldn't be ready for several days, especially if it needed any new parts.

"Oh, that's perfect." Andrea's delight echoed through the telephone lines. "Remember Paul, the good-looking, sandy-haired guy you met at lunch, the one that all the guys were teasing? Well, he's really been wanting to ask you out but hasn't been able to. Why don't I have him pick you up and bring you to the party? Who knows? You two just might hit it off."

"Andrea, I don't know."

"Jennifer, so help me, if you don't get out some, you're going to wind up an old prune like … Miss Baker." Both girls giggled like teenagers again as they remembered their teacher of long ago.

"You know, I hadn't thought of her in years. Wonder what ever happened to her? You know, we really were rough on her."

"You're right; we were, and I'd like to take back some of the awful things we said and did but … we can't. We can just make sure that you don't turn out the same way. I'll tell Paul to pick you up Saturday about six thirty, and no more excuses."

"Andr—" The click of the receiver was her only response.

Jennifer groaned as she replaced the telephone and slumped into the overstuffed armchair next to the table. A party was the last place she wanted to be, and with a group of strangers too.

But at least strangers might be better than a party of people who thought they knew what had been happening at the mill.

Jennifer dressed casually for the party, not really caring if anyone took notice of her. It was almost 6:30 before she put the finishing touches on her hair and makeup, but she saw no sign of her date. Secretly she hoped he wouldn't show at all.

Jennifer groaned as she heard the doorbell ring. *Nothing in this town has gone my way yet; why should it start now?* she mused to herself as she turned off the light in her room and made her way down the stairway.

With a forced smile on her face, Jennifer was puzzled by the look of disapproval she received from her mother, who exited the room as soon as her daughter arrived, leaving the two young people alone. Mrs. Kent had never expressed an opinion about any of the boys her daughter had dated, probably because Mr. Kent has always told them his opinion about each one. Jennifer smiled as she remembered some of their heated discussions, but he had never been wrong about any of them.

A strong, offensive smell of liquor filtered through the room as Jennifer greeted her guest.

"You look as pretty as I remember, Miss Kent." Paul's smile did not quite reach his eyes, giving his words an insincere tone.

"Just call me Jennifer, Paul. Well, are you ready to go?" Jennifer asked as she reached for her jacket and purse and headed for the door, not allowing her date the chance to answer.

The ride to Andrea's was filled with unimportant small talk, as Jennifer found herself paying extra attention to the road, a growing concern for their welfare becoming more apparent with each passing mile. A sigh of relief slipped from her lips as they pulled into the already-crowded driveway of the Combest home.

"Jennifer, I'm so glad you made it." Andrea greeted her guests warmly as she ushered them through the door. "I really thought you'd find a way to back out," Andrea whispered for only Jennifer to hear.

"The thought did cross my mind," Jennifer confessed.

"Listen, I apologize for Paul's condition, but they closed the season today down at the fire station, and some of the guys started celebrating a little early. If he gets too bad, we'll take care of him."

"Don't worry about it; I can take care of myself."

The music blared loud with a heavy metal beat that throbbed through Jennifer's head. The crush of all the people crowded into the confines of the small house soon became overwhelming. She quietly slipped out the kitchen door into the cool darkness of the night.

"Too much for you too?" The deep voice was easily recognizable.

"What are you doing here?" Jennifer asked, somewhat irritated not only that Jarrod was at the party but also because he had seemed to have had the same idea of escape that she had.

"Here at the party or here by the tree?" he asked teasingly. "I'm at the party because I was invited, and I'm out here for probably the same reason you are."

"Hey, Jenny, you out here? There you are." Paul slightly stumbled as he came down the steps of the house and draped his arm around her shoulders in an all-too-friendly manner.

"Maybe we didn't come out here for the same reason." Jarrod's words held a twinge of disappointment as he turned suddenly and returned to the party inside the house.

"Who's that guy?" Paul demanded. "I thought you were my date."

"I think it's time to go home, Paul," Jennifer stated firmly as she removed his arm from around her shoulder.

"Why so early—so you can go and meet your boyfriend?"

"That's enough! I don't have to explain anything to you." Jennifer turned to walk away.

"My dates don't walk away from me," Paul shouted as he grabbed Jennifer's arm and pulled her into his arms.

"Let go of me! You're drunk!"

"But I'll still be the best you've ever had," Paul boasted as he tightened his grip around Jennifer's back.

"Well then I'll just have to settle for second best," Jennifer firmly retorted.

Just then a group of fellow firefighters came around the corner of the building carrying an ice chest full of beer.

"Hey, Paul, come on, just got in a new supply."

"I'll be back, and you'd better be here," Paul threatened as he released Jennifer from his grip and ambled over to join his buddies.

"I wouldn't bet on it," Jennifer muttered under her breath.

As soon as possible, Jennifer made her way through the crowd and out the front door of the house. Taking a deep breath, she began walking down the dark country road. Gravel crunched beneath her high-heeled shoes as she occasionally stumbled over unseen pebbles.

The sound of an approaching vehicle on the deserted stretch of road quickened her heart as she realized the foolishness of her actions.

A flash of headlights temporarily blinded her as a truck came around the bend. Slowing down as it approached the pedestrian, the vehicle slowly passed her and then came to a stop as the driver shifted gears and began backing up in Jennifer's direction. Panic began to grip her as she watched the unknown person come closer, her fast walk quickly becoming a run.

Suddenly, the unknown driver was bathed in the light of another vehicle and sped off in the opposite direction, throwing rocks and dirt in his wake.

"Are you okay?"

Jennifer almost wept tears of joy and relief at the sound of Jarrod's deep voice.

"Yes, I'm fine." Jennifer smiled her relief.

"Good! See you around." His voice was calm and casual as he began to slowly drive away.

"Jarrod, don't you dare leave me here!" Jennifer yelled at the departing vehicle.

The brake lights flashed as Jennifer ran to the passenger's side of the truck.

"I got the impression you really didn't want me around," Jarrod said innocently.

"Well, sometimes ... impressions can be wrong."

The cover of darkness hid the smile that brightened Jarrod's face as they drove in silence down the dark, solitary country road.

The sounds of pots and pans in the kitchen so early in the morning caused Jennifer to groan and snuggle deeper into the warm covers of her bed. Still the sounds of activity in other parts of the house insisted on disturbing her from any further attempts at snatching even a few minutes more of much-needed sleep.

It had been well after two o'clock before Jennifer had made it home; if it hadn't been for Jarrod's help, it would have been much later.

At last giving up completely, she grudgingly threw back the covers, stood beside the bed, and lazily stretched to try and bring some life back into her weary body. Grabbing her ancient winter robe, she slipped into the equally dilapidated matching slippers and made her way down the stairs and toward the kitchen.

The sound of her mother's pleasant laughter and the smell of fresh coffee and bacon caught Jennifer by surprise as she crossed the dining room and opened the swinging door into the kitchen area. Mrs. Kent was seated comfortably on a stool at the counter area enjoying a cup of morning coffee. Much to Jennifer's astonishment, there at the stove, aptly flipping pancakes above the griddle, stood Jarrod. The sleeves of his dress shirt were rolled up past his elbows, and around his chest was one of Mrs. Kent's larger aprons tied securely with a bow in the center of his back.

"What are you doing here?"

"Jennifer, watch your manners; you know that's no way for a lady to treat a guest," scolded Mrs. Kent.

Briefly throwing her mother a frown, Jennifer once again returned to question Jarrod. It just wasn't fair. He had received less sleep than she had, and yet somehow he managed to look completely rested and refreshed. Before she could continue her inquiry, Jarrod pointed the spatula he was holding in his hand toward her and teasingly threatened.

"Now you remember what your mother said."

"Excuse me, Mr. Drake, may I ask what you're doing here, especially this time of the morning?" Jennifer asked with mock formality.

"I invited him over for breakfast since he invited us to accompany him to church this morning," Mrs. Kent interjected pleasantly. "I hope you don't mind, dear?"

"What choice do I have, but why didn't you warn me so I could have made other arrangements?" Jennifer retorted.

"Now, now, don't be so hospitable or I might get the idea you enjoy having me around," Jarrod remarked as he turned to check on the progress of breakfast. "If you hurry you just might be able to make yourself presentable in time to have breakfast with the rest of us. Or is that the best you can do this early in the morning? If it is, I really feel sorry for anyone who might have to face you every morning."

"I'm sorry, but this is the best I can do on such short notice," Jennifer replied, reaching into the cupboard for a coffee cup. Then she poured herself a generous amount of the fragrant brew and crossed the small open space of the crowded room made even smaller by Jarrod's presence. Sitting down at the table, she silently challenged anyone to further criticize her attire or actions. Gingerly sipping the hot contents of her cup, she watched with demure interest the other occupants of the room, especially the skillful chef.

Mrs. Kent chattered with Jarrod. Both appeared to have forgotten the brooding presence of the young woman seated quietly at the table.

At long last the tantalizing fare was ready. Jarrod held Mrs. Kent's chair and waited for her to be seated before taking a place at the head of the table. Jennifer was stunned to see another male sitting in the chair her father had always occupied.

"What's the matter, Jennifer? You look like you've seen a ghost." Mrs. Kent touched her daughter's arm as she spoke with concern.

"Oh, nothing, Mom, I was just ... never mind." Jennifer replied as she forked the food that had been placed on her plate.

"I'm beginning to think you have something against eating when I'm around. If I remember right, you played with your food when we went to Eureka," Jarrod mentioned as he took Mrs. Kent's hand in his and bowed his head, also offering Jennifer an outstretched hand.

Jennifer paused before she laid her hand in Jarrod's and listened to his heartfelt prayer.

"Why didn't you tell me about this yesterday?" Jennifer questioned her mother as soon as the prayer was finished. "Or for that matter, you could have said something last night." She threw an accusing look at Jarrod.

"Well, dear, this was kind of sudden. I saw Jarrod at the market last night, and he offered to accompany us to church today, so I just invited him over for breakfast this morning. Remember how your father used to always get up and try to prepare Sunday-morning breakfast for us and most of the time we had to bail him out, and we would wind up with a horrible mess in the kitchen." The smile on Mrs. Kent's face and the laughter in her voice did not quite hide the trace of sadness that dulled her otherwise sparkling eyes as she recalled happy memories from her past.

"As for me," Jarrod interjected, "it didn't seem worth mentioning; besides, you seemed rather busy last night or at least had other things on your mind." His eyes sparkled as he watched Jennifer's cheeks heighten in color as his teasing hit its mark.

"My, my, are you sure that's the best you can do early in the morning?" Jarrod inquired as his hand felt the threadbare sleeve of her robe.

Jennifer stiffened at the subtle touch, chiding herself for even noticing. "This happens to be very comfortable and warm." Jennifer pulled the collar of the garment tighter around her throat. "Besides, it doesn't really look all that bad."

Jarrod shrugged his shoulders, as if it made no difference to him at all.

"You were right; you really can cook," Jennifer offered in an effort to restore conversation around the table.

A low chuckle rose from the head of the table as Jarrod watched Jennifer. "Have I ever lied to you?"

Jennifer sat puzzled for a moment. *No, he has never lied to me. Is he hinting that maybe the same isn't true of me?* Her mind was a maze of questions with no answers, of emotions that knew no foundation.

"Jennifer, we'd better hurry if we're going to be on time for church." Mrs. Kent broke into Jennifer's thoughts and brought her daughter back into the circle of conversation taking place around the tiny kitchen table.

"Mom, I'm—" Jennifer began to try to find some excuse not to accompany her two breakfast companions to the morning worship services, but Jarrod guessed her intentions and cut her off before she even had a chance to think of a logical excuse.

"Now, you wouldn't want people to start talking about your mom and me, would you? Just think what a field day this town would have if I were to accompany this respectable lady to church unchaperoned," Jarrod teased as he winked in Mrs. Kent's direction. Jennifer had not seen her mother blush with enjoyment since ... her father would tease her out of an angry mood whenever they had a disagreement.

"That is, unless you're afraid to be seen with me," Jarrod whispered so only Jennifer could hear.

"Why should I be afraid of you?" Jennifer protested as she pushed her chair away from the table and carried her dishes to the sink. "If you will excuse me, I have to get ready."

As she showered and curled her hair, Jennifer felt turmoil building within her heart. It had been a long time since she had been to church. And she hadn't been to the church she had grown up in since her father's death. The memories were still clear—all the activities of her youth, the Bible contests she had won, speaking tournaments, the offices of responsibility she had held ... everything seemed like just yesterday. Everyone had always used her faithfulness as an example for others to follow. But nobody knew her secret, nobody but her dad. Jennifer brushed away a gentle tear that slid down her cheek. How would she ever have the strength to walk back into that building and know deep in her heart that everything had been a lie? She had not done the things she had because she loved the Lord but rather because it was what she felt others had expected of her.

"Jarrod was right," Jennifer said to her reflection in the mirror.

"Jennifer, hurry up or we'll be late," Mrs. Kent called from the bottom of the stairs.

"I'll be there in a minute," Jennifer called back as she took a deep breath and straightened her shoulders to face whatever lay ahead.

Mrs. Kent was in the hallway when Jennifer descended the stairs, and Jarrod was just helping her mom into her coat. As soon as he finished helping Mrs. Kent, he took the coat Jennifer had worn to Eureka from the closet and held it open for her to slip into.

"Have I told you that you look lovely this morning?" Jarrod murmured against her ear as the coat came to rest on her shoulders.

Jennifer felt the acceleration of her heart as she inhaled the subtle richness of his cologne and felt the warmth of his breath on her hair. The sincerity of his compliment and the resolve in his voice stole the essence of life from her lungs.

"If I remember correctly, you complained about how awful I looked this morning," Jennifer countered in an effort to bring her own emotions under control.

"Remind me to have my eyes examined," Jarrod replied as he brought her under the protective shelter of his arm and massaged her shoulder with his hand. Jennifer closed her eyes to hold back the tears that once again threatened. *It would be so easy for me to come to love this man—this man who only seems interested in being my friend.*

When they reached the driveway, Jennifer was surprised to see one of the company trucks instead of his automobile.

"Hope you don't mind if we take the truck, but my car is being repaired; seems it had a little misunderstanding with a rock," Jarrod said to Mrs. Kent as an apology while he held open the door of the vehicle for the ladies.

"We can take my car," Jennifer offered.

"No, thanks, but your car would be a little on the cramped side for me, and besides, I thought it was in the garage." Jarrod raised an eyebrow as he waited for Jennifer's response.

"Well, it *was* in the garage yesterday, but they finished with it sooner than expected," Jennifer reported as she nudged her mother ahead, hoping she would take the center of the bench seat, thus leaving the space next to the door for herself. After Mrs. Kent entered the vehicle, Jarrod closed the door, and taking Jennifer by the elbow, led her to the driver's side. The frown that crossed his face promised her she would be sorry if she made any attempt to thwart his intentions. Jennifer returned his promise with a scowl of her own as she climbed into the waiting pickup and was rewarded with a deep chuckle from her adversary and a knowing smile from her mother.

The ride to the church was fast, but Jennifer found that her head was pounding from the deep concentration required for her to remain aloof and unaffected by the almost-overpowering magnetism she felt toward the man seated so close, within the confines of the truck.

Once they reached the church, Jarrod played the part of the perfect gentleman, taking each of the ladies by the elbow and walking between them down the center aisle of the historic sanctuary to a seat near the front.

Jennifer sat quietly as various people stopped to chat with either her mother or Jarrod, offering only the briefest of responses to any query directed to her.

The muscular arm stretched across the back of the pew sent waves of heat down her back wherever it briefly touched her. As the service began and the congregation stood for the first song, Jarrod's hand unerringly found the curve of her waist and rested there throughout the entire hymn.

Jennifer was surprised by the rich tenor voice coming from the person standing next to her. The pleasant tones blended easily with the alto of her mother's clear voice and the lead of her own attractive voice whenever she was able to focus her attention long enough to find the correct notes and words.

Jennifer could feel the tension mounting as the service progressed. She shifted uncomfortably as the minister stood and opened his Bible. Hoping that the morning's sermon would be on giving or some other subject she could fairly easily block out, Jennifer felt her disappointment as the minister announced his text to be John 17.

Jennifer had not realized just how long it had been since she had opened her Bible, and the pastor had already finished his opening comments before she found the Scripture.

"Jesus loves us so much that his last prayer was not for Himself but for us—that we would know *the only way* to have eternal life is by knowing and accepting the only true God.

"We can't forgive ourselves of any wrongdoing; only God can do that. No matter how hard we may try, nothing we can do will make any difference at all.

"It all sounds so easy, but how can we be sure? Jesus said, 'Behold I stand at the door and knock if any man will hear my voice and open the door, I will come in to him and will sup with him and he with me.'

"Titus 1:2 tells us God cannot lie. Now if Jesus said this, can He lie?"

"No," a number of people from the congregation answered.

"That's right! Jesus said it, and He cannot lie. What He said would happen in your life if you invited Him in is true, and that settles it."

Jennifer shifted on the hard seat. The minister made it all sound so easy, just as Jarrod had. *So why does it seem so hard for me to accept?* Questions swirled around in her head, but she found no peace in her troubled heart.

She was surprised when Jarrod nudged her elbow as the rest of the congregation stood for the closing hymn. She had been so caught up in her own world of doubts and confusion that the rest of the sermon had slipped by without her hearing any of it.

Jarrod's face reflected concern as he studied her troubled face, but Jennifer pretended interest in the words they were singing and ignored him as best she could.

When the service ended, Jennifer breathed a sigh of relief, but the escape she sought was not yet at hand as Jarrod firmly held her elbow within his grip and purposely stopped and chatted with everyone who spoke to them, prolonging her ordeal.

"Jennifer!"

Relief swept through her as Andrea approached the trio and they headed toward the parking lot.

"I need to talk to you a minute." Andrea's distressed look silently pleaded with Jarrod and Mrs. Kent to allow her to talk to Jennifer alone.

"We'll meet you at the truck, dear," Mrs. Kent offered after glancing at Jarrod. "But don't be too long, we're having company for dinner."

Andrea waited until the others were out of listening distance before she turned to Jennifer. "Listen, I'm really sorry about what happened the other night. I didn't know Paul was such a jerk. The guys said he had just broken up with the girl he had gone with for a long time and was kind of taking it all out on you. I'm really sorry, Jen."

"Don't worry about it. It's not your fault." Jennifer tried to assure her friend.

"I'm sure glad Jarrod was there to see you got home okay though. Boy was he upset when he couldn't find you. Come to think of it, why did you do such a stupid thing anyway? Lots of people there would have given you a ride home. You could even have borrowed my car."

"I just wanted to be alone and think for a while." Jennifer shrugged her shoulders casually. "It's not that far into town."

"You idiot, it doesn't have to be far for something to happen. This is not the same place it was when we were young."

"Is your lecture over? I think I'm big enough to take care of myself."

"Jen, I didn't mean to lecture you, but I am concerned, please believe that."

"I didn't mean to be so sharp, Andrea, I just have a lot on my mind."

"Like Dr. Drake?" Andrea teased.

"No!" Jennifer snapped and stared to walk away.

"Jennifer, I'm really sorry. I was only teasing," Andrea apologized.

"I'm just a little touchy lately, okay? Let's just drop the subject."

"Okay, and I promise I'll try and keep my nose out of your life."

Jennifer hugged her friend. "I'll call you later this week."

"Promise?"

"Yes, I promise, and everything is fine."

"Listen, I've got to go; Dan's in the car. See you later." Andrea waved to her friend as she ran across the lawn of the little country church to her car.

Jennifer watched as Andrea greeted her waiting husband even though they had only been apart for a few minutes. As she walked to the parking lot, Jennifer wondered if she would ever know the happiness her friend had found.

"I was beginning to think we were going to have to send out a search party," Jarrod teased when Jennifer reached the waiting pickup.

"Afraid I'd run away again?"

"Ouch!" Jarrod faked a painful wound.

"Who are we having over for dinner?" Jennifer directed her question to her mother, ignoring Jarrod's antics.

"Well, I thought if Jarrod didn't have any plans for this afternoon, he could stay and join us," Mrs. Kent said, catching the full force of her daughter's disapproving look, but the older woman was not the least bit intimidated by her actions.

"I must admit the offer sounds good, but I don't want to be a bother to anyone or make a nuisance of myself."

"Don't be silly. We'd love to have you, and you won't be any problem at all. Will he, Jennifer?"

Jennifer bit the inside of her lip to hold back the words she was tempted to express but instead just sighed reluctantly, knowing she would not be able to excuse herself from Jarrod's company without hurting her mother's feelings. Pasting a syrupy smile on her face, she offered her own assurances that it would be no problem for him to come to lunch.

Once they were in the house, Jennifer busied herself with the preparations for the Sunday luncheon. From the well-stocked cupboards, it was apparent her mother had planned on having company join them during their noon meal all along.

She was capable of taking care of her own personal life without anyone playing Cupid for her, Jennifer thought with bitterness as she peeled the potatoes with more force than needed, suddenly taking a small nick of flesh out of her thumb. The sharp pain only intensified the anger and frustration she felt about her present situation.

Garden peas and a tossed salad accompanied the crisp golden fried chicken and mashed potatoes with gravy. For dessert, Mrs. Kent brought out one of her delicious, fresh baked apple pies, topped with ice cream. Mrs. Kent had refused to allow Jarrod to assist in preparing the meal and banished him to the living room until the meal was completed.

When Jennifer went to call him to join them at the dining table, she found him reclining comfortably on the couch, minus his jacket and tie, watching a football game on the television, making himself right at home. Despite herself, Jennifer felt a warm, pleasant glow spread over her as she stood and watched the animated changes taking place across his face at the enthusiasm he expressed watching the game, like a little boy caught up in the excitement of the competition. Her heart soared as she regarded with pleasure this man who was so confident of himself that he could relax and enjoy himself no matter where he was.

The meal turned out to be a more pleasant experience than Jennifer had anticipated, and she soon found herself not only relaxing but also taking part in and enjoying the refreshing conversation taking place around her.

Jarrod insisted on helping the ladies clear the table and clean the dishes, and after only a small amount of fussing, Mrs. Kent relented and allowed him to help.

Jennifer felt the twinges of loneliness surface as Jarrod began to gather his belongings.

"You haven't even finished the game yet," Mrs. Kent protested.

"I really to have to get going, Thelma. Thanks so much for lunch and the wonderful company. I really have enjoyed myself." Turning to Jennifer, Jarrod's dark eyes sparkled as his smile brightened his entire face. "I do hope it wasn't too much of an ordeal having me here today."

"Don't be silly, we've enjoyed having you." Jennifer granted the small triumph.

Jarrod stood for a long moment before he spoke. "Thanks again, next time will be my treat." He bent and kissed Mrs. Kent on the forehead and then turned to Jennifer and put his arm around her shoulder. "Why don't you walk me to the truck?"

Jarrod had asked but didn't bother waiting for an answer as he began walking toward the door, bringing Jennifer along with him.

Once they were outside, Jarrod remained silent until they reached his company pickup. "Jennifer, are you okay? You seemed a little upset at church."

Pasting a pleasant smile on her face, Jennifer was surprised at the weakness of her voice. "I'm fine. I ... just hadn't been to that church since Dad's funeral." *Nor any church, for that matter,* she added silently to herself.

"You're sure? If you ever want to talk, just remember I'm a very good listener."

For a moment Jennifer thought—hoped—Jarrod was going to take her in his arms and kiss her. She only prayed her disappointment didn't show on her face when he squeezed her shoulder and turned to climb into the cab of the truck.

"See you tomorrow at work." His casual comments felt alike a slam in the face to Jennifer as he backed out of the driveway.

Jennifer stood watching the vehicle disappear around the corner, stunned by his indifference toward her.

CHAPTER

10

Jennifer was not surprised by the sudden change in the weather as winter caught Round Valley in its cold grip. The brisk or gentle rainy days of autumn were replaced by the mottled gray clouds that now hung low over the valley, trapping the cold beneath its cover. Whiffs of smoke from fireplaces and burning leaves settled into streaks below the encasing clouds. Temperatures dropped below freezing during the night to raise only a few degrees during the daylight hours.

Each season in the countryside was marked by definite changes. Jennifer stared in fascination at the sparkling light show taking place before her as she paused beside the protective windbreak of a log deck. Because of the brittle nature of pine, the new-cut logs were stacked apart from the rest of the unfinished wood and covered with a water sprinkling system in both winter and summer to keep them from splitting. The sudden change in the weather had transformed the ugly, water-soaked logs into beautiful, shimmering cascades of frozen waterfalls and icicles.

Sparkling beams of light danced from one ice-bound trickle of water to another, leaving a mirage of tiny multi-colored rainbows in its path.

The intermittent gusts of wind sent thousands of glassy fragments descending to the frozen earth—a clear, musical symphony audible only for a few brief moments before it became lost in the hustle and noise surrounding it.

Pulling her collar closer to her ears, Jennifer smiled at the island of beauty she had found among the sounds and ugliness around her. Gazing at the beauty she saw, Jennifer pondered the complexity of the events that had beset her once-calm and -comfortable world, changing it in a way that could never be recovered and once again make it the way it had once been. *Maybe it is time to forget about the past and go on with whatever the future holds.* Jennifer smiled at the thought. *If only it were that easy. Too many events from the past have to be settled once and for all before I can ever go on and someday find happiness again.*

When she had come home to the valley, she was hurting and angry. But her anger was directed to only one source—*God.* God had taken her father away from her. He had also caused the broken relationship that had developed between her and her dad. At least that was the way it seemed at the time, but now nothing seemed clear. And now the longings of her heart told her that maybe—just maybe—her dad had been right.

And there was the little matter of Jarrod! Sometimes he acted like he really cared about her, and then there seemed to be an invisible wall between them. At other times he acted more like a friend than a would-be lover. No matter how he truly felt about her, one thing was certain: there would always be a part of her heart that would love Jarrod. She had at last admitted the one truth she was sure of: she did love Jarrod.

The most important element in any relationship was trust. Until Jarrod understood that she had nothing to do with the thefts at the mill, she had no hope he would ever return her feelings for him.

In any small community, it is difficult to keep secrets, and Round Valley was no exception. Lately the favorite topic of conversation was the recent events at the mill. Glen, although a recent arrival to the valley, had acquired a number of acquaintances but no close friends. Speculations concerning his associates in the daring attempt at thievery were high on the list of discussions.

Most people expressed relief that the recent fire had done so little damage to the valley's primary source of employment. It would have been a very dismal winter had the mill been forced to shut down its operations, even for a short time.

Crossing the almost-vacant yard, Jennifer headed for the main office. She was determined to find out how the investigation concerning Glen was progressing.

"Hi, Andrea," Jennifer said, her voice expressing warmth to her old friend as she entered the cozy office area. "I can't believe it's turned cold so fast."

"I know what you mean. We actually had to turn on our furnace last night," Andrea noted with a shiver.

"You don't happen to have any nice, hot coffee around here anywhere, do you?"

"Only what's left in the pot, and I'm sure it's pretty strong by now."

"Oh, that's okay; I just want to warm my hands holding the cup," Jennifer teased as she removed her gloves and poured a cup of the hot brew. "Say, have you heard anything about Glen?" Jennifer hoped her voice sounded casual and disinterested as she waited for Andrea's answer.

"No, I haven't heard anything definite, just the same old rumors that everyone's heard. But Mr. Drake did have the deputy in his office for a long time this morning and asked not to be disturbed at all. He sure wasn't too pleased after it was all over, let me tell you."

"Did he say what was wrong?" Jennifer blew into the thick black liquid to avoid Andrea's eyes.

"No, right after the deputy left he came out and said he had some errands to run and left. Haven't heard from him all afternoon, and that's really not like him."

"Andrea ..." Jennifer paused before she continued, not liking the way her thoughts were leading her, "what kind of business volume has Mr. Drake been doing lately?"

"Business is great. Why? You don't think you'll be laid off work or something, do you?"

"No, I was just wondering, with all his new expansion, if Mr. Drake wasn't in a financial bind or the like."

"And would steal from himself?" A hard-as-steel voice came from Jarrod's office door.

Jennifer jumped at the sound and spilled the burning liquid onto her hands and coat. Andrea was also surprised and accidentally knocked several papers off her desk, sending them sprawling across the wooden floor.

"Mr. Drake, I didn't know you were back. When did you come in?" Andrea was having trouble concealing her embarrassment as she quizzed her boss and tried to retrieve the raft of papers from the floor.

"As you can see, I'm here, and I've been here long enough." His eyes never left Jennifer as he spoke to his secretary. "If you're so interested in my financial condition, Miss Kent, would you like to see last quarter's reports?"

"No, thank you. A good accountant can make reports say just about whatever he or his client wishes." Jennifer tried to sound calm and collected and hoped her pounding heart and constricting throat didn't reveal her nervousness.

"I think we should continue this conversation in my office, if you don't mind." Jarrod's face remained grim as he stepped aside and motioned for Jennifer to enter his office.

Jennifer walked instead over to the sink and dumped the remaining coffee before following Jarrod's command and assumed a ramrod posture and strolled past his statuesque figure, into his office.

She winced as the door slammed shut; the mill owner was unmistakably agitated as he proceeded to the chair behind his desk.

"I think we need to get a couple of issues straight here and now. There is no way I'm going to steal from my own company! I've worked hard to build this place into what it is now, and I'm not about to risk everything on something so stupid!"

"Just because you say it's so, you think I should believe you? If I remember correctly, we've had a couple of presidents tell us they weren't lying either, and guess what? They lied like the

Devil himself. So you expect me to believe you just because *you* say it's true. Besides, who else would have the most to gain by this?" Jennifer stood her ground, sounding much more confident than she felt. "Why should I believe a word you say when you don't believe anything I say?"

Jarrod stared at her for a long time before he released a weary sigh and slumped down in his chair. "I guess I had that coming, didn't I? I'm not sure who or what to believe anymore."

Jennifer sat down in the chair in front of the large desk and laughed out loud at her own thoughts. "Would you believe I, of all people, almost asked you to remember your faith in God?"

Jarrod's weary expression softened as a warm smile crossed his face and pleasure shone deep in his dark eyes. "At least that's a good sign."

Jennifer took a deep breath before she responded. "I guess it is."

"I wanted to talk to you after church last Sunday, but you didn't seem quite ready yet."

"No, I'm still not ready, but let's not get off the subject." Jennifer hurried on, wanting to draw the conversation away from herself. "I have no reason to run the risk of stealing from you and getting caught either. This sure points out how little we know about each other, doesn't it?"

"Well, what are we going to do about it?"

"I don't know about you, but I'm going to find out what's going on around here if for no other reason than to clear my own name, and we'll just see what happens." Jennifer stood and looked at Jarrod, hoping he would give her some reason or assurance that he wasn't involved and that he truly believed her innocence.

"Want some help?" Jarrod offered as he stood pushing his chair back with his legs.

Jennifer thought for a long second before she answered. "Thanks, but this is something I'm going to have to do on my own ..."

"You mean if I'm involved I might mess things up on purpose if we worked together."

"I guess that's exactly what I mean."

"Jennifer ... how did we ever mess things up so badly that we don't even trust each other anymore?"

"Did we ever have any reason to trust each other?"

Jennifer had no idea where to start her search for the truth and tried to remember every detail of the events leading up to Glen's arrest. Nothing made sense; some vague, distant memory lingered on the fringe of her senses but not close enough to be recalled.

She carefully walked the area where they had encountered Glen and his accomplice, hoping to find some overlooked clue to the identity of the unknown person.

Dejected and cold, the lonesome figure made her way across the frozen ground to the warmth of the company lunchroom. No matter how many times she reviewed the information available on the thefts, nothing made sense. She hoped with all her heart that Jarrod was not involved, but who else would have a reason, unless someone was out to take over or destroy Drake Lumber? Jennifer brightened at this prospect. Maybe Bradley would be able to shed some light on this theory ... but she'd have to be cautious when she talked to him because the two might be in on this together or Bradley might let Jarrod know she'd been asking questions concerning him.

Jennifer Kent! I'm surprised at you! Next thing you know you'll be suspecting your own mother! She looked around, hoping no one had heard her talking to herself. The idea did bring up another problem though; until this whole matter was solved, she would have to be very careful about what she said to her mother, since Jarrod had won her mother's respect and admiration in the months since her father's death. Whatever she mentioned could and most likely would make its way back to Jarrod.

For the first time in her life, Jennifer felt truly alone. She could trust no one and had no one to turn to for advice. *Oh, God, what am I going to do?* Stopping mid-stride, Jennifer turned her eyes toward the bleak gray sky and let the wind blow her soft, wavy hair off her face.

"God, it finally looks like it's just You and me. I have no one else to turn to. Please help me." Jennifer stood watching as the clouds rolled by. Slowly she resumed her trek across the yard. She had received no assurance that the matter would be resolved, no new inspirations about what was happening to her world, no sudden peace in her heart. Nothing seemed to have changed; all was just the same! Jennifer shook her head as she entered the lunchroom, feeling disappointed but not really sure what she had been expecting in the first place.

"Jennifer ..." Mrs. Kent seemed hesitant to proceed with her train of thought as she looked deep into her first cup of morning coffee.

Jennifer noticed the pause in her mother's voice and glanced up from the newspaper. "Yes, Mother?"

"I was just wondering, dear, if you'd mind if ... Reverend Kelly dropped by to visit with us later this week."

Jennifer studied her mother's creased brow; the older woman had never hesitated to invite people over to the house in the past, and she was a little surprised by her mother's sudden concern for her daughter's feelings.

"Why should I mind who you have over?"

"Well, dear, the reason he wanted to stop by is that Jarrod seemed concerned about your reaction to the sermon on Sunday and felt you might like to talk to someone about it."

"If he's so concerned, why doesn't he just talk to me about it himself?" Jennifer felt her spine stiffen at the mention of Jarrod's name and was more than a little miffed that he had not had the courage to talk to her himself about the situation. But to be honest, he had brought up the subject in his office and she had informed him she wasn't ready to talk yet.

"Well, honey, I think he feels you might not listen to him for some reason. You two haven't had another argument, have you? I do wish you two would get your differences worked out." Mrs. Kent's voice had a wishful quality about it that made it sound almost like she was hoping for something that Jennifer felt sure would never come to pass.

"Mother, there's nothing to settle between us. Jarrod Drake simply does not trust me and feels I'm a liar and a thief, and that's all there is to it."

"Jennifer, you don't really believe that now, do you? If he felt that way, why would he want the preacher to come and talk to you?"

"I really don't know, nor do I care. Maybe he's just one of those fanatical Christians that feel it's his personal obligation to see that everyone in the world becomes a Christian too." Jennifer couldn't help the trace of sarcasm from slipping into her voice.

"Jennifer, are you really that bitter toward God?"

"Mom, I'm not bitter. Why should I be—because He took my father away when he had a chance to relax and begin to enjoy life a little bit?" Throwing down the paper, she stormed to the sink to dump the remainder of her coffee.

"Do you think you're the only one who misses your father? You seem to forget that he was my husband longer than he was your father." Mrs. Kent's words were thick with emotion as she spoke. "Did you know your father had cancer? No, I didn't think you did." Mrs. Kent paused as she saw the color drain from her daughter's face. "He had found out only a few weeks before he died and—before you ask—no, they couldn't treat it and he knew that. Your father was a man who had lived all his life out of doors and to have slowly withered up to a mere shell of what he had been would have been hell for him. So you see, the heart attack was a blessing in disguise. It was just the way he wanted to go, quickly, with no regrets." Mrs. Kent's eyes were brimming with unshed tears as she held her head up and looked at her daughter.

Jennifer's voice was just a whisper. "Mom, I didn't know. I'm so sorry."

Mrs. Kent stood and began clearing away the breakfast dishes. "Well, now you do."

Crossing the room, Jennifer embraced her mother. "Please forgive me; I've really been selfish lately, haven't I?"

"At times you have been a little difficult to get along with." Her smile helped relieve some of the tension that filled the small room.

"Go ahead and have the preacher over, but you make sure you're there too. I'm not ready to talk to him by myself yet."

"Okay, I'll make the appointment but ... please try to talk to Jarrod. I know he's really been concerned about you."

Jennifer bit her lip to hold back the stinging remark she was about to make. "I'll see if I can find out what's going on."

Her mother's smile of encouragement was worth the pain. "I'm so glad. I just know everything will work out for the best."

Mrs. Kent made the appointment with the minister much sooner than Jennifer had hoped for, and she soon found herself trying to think up excuses not to be around at the scheduled hour but without success.

Groaning as the doorbell rang, Jennifer made her way down the stairs and into the living room while her mother was busy taking their guest's coat and offering him a cup of coffee.

The minister was a very nondescript middle-aged man with a pleasant enough face and friendly voice, but Jennifer still felt an invisible wall had been erected between them, even if it was her own doing.

"Jennifer, I realize we haven't had a chance to get to know each other very well yet, but I've heard many nice compliments about you. I'm sure we'll be friends very soon."

"Just what have you heard about me?" Jennifer couldn't control the iciness that tinged her words as she spoke.

It was easy to see the older gentleman was taken aback by the coolness of her attitude toward him and stumbled over his words. "Just about ... how you were quite a good leader when you were growing up and ... that ..."

"That I now have some serious doubts about my faith. That I might be a thief, that ... should I go on?" Jennifer stared at the sunned man still standing in the middle of the living room.

"Jennifer, haven't you even offered the reverend a chair yet?" Mrs. Kent asked as she returned to her guest with three cups of coffee on a shiny silver serving tray.

"Sorry, Mom, but we've been talking, and I haven't had a chance yet," she said sweetly.

"Thank you, Mrs. Kent." The minister took a cup of coffee from his hostess and used the few seconds to regroup his thoughts before continuing with the conversation.

"We really enjoyed your sermon on Sunday, Reverend," Mrs. Kent continued, unaware of the tense undercurrent circling the room around her.

"It was nice to see you all there, especially you, Miss Kent." The minister directed his response to a silent Jennifer. "Mr. Drake said you'd been working on the weekends and hadn't been able to attend the services."

"What else did Jarrod tell you?"

The minister paused before he spoke. "Only that he had been counseling with you and felt it was time for someone with more experienced to take over."

"I'm that big a problem, huh!"

"No! Mr. Drake just felt you might be a little more receptive if someone else were to talk to you instead of him."

"Just what did he say my problem was?"

"Only that you were questioning the sincerity of your beliefs."

"That's putting it mildly." Jennifer's reply was laced with sarcasm.

"Mrs. Kent, do you mind if we have a word of prayer?"

"Not at all." Mrs. Kent glanced from her daughter to the minister, puzzled by the strange and tense conversation they were conducting.

The prayer was brief, and the rest of the minister's visit was even shorter. Jennifer answered any questions put to her with curt replies.

Mrs. Kent leaned against the door after saying good-bye to the minister. "Would you mind telling me what was going on here this afternoon? I felt like an outsider in my own house. Jennifer Kent, I have never seen you so rude to any guest in this house as you were today unless it was to Jarrod last Sunday morning. What has gotten into you, child?"

"Nothing was going on, Mother. I just wish people would quit trying to help me solve my problems. I'll work them out in my own way."

"Jennifer, don't you know they only care about you and want to help?"

"Are you telling me Jarrod cares about *me* or only about my poor unsaved soul? Well, my soul and I are doing just fine, thank you, and you can tell that to Mr. Drake the next time you talk to him."

Jennifer stubbornly pushed herself up from her chair and walked out of the room, not feeling very proud of either her words or actions.

CHAPTER
. . . .
11
. . . .

Almost everyone around the mill was beginning to accept the security force into the inner circle of friendship. They were being included in the joking and teasing camaraderie that interspersed the daily work routine. On this particular shift, everyone seemed to be in a very jovial mood as Jennifer walked up the steps of the lunch room to join a small group of workers laughing and talking over their first coffee break of the afternoon. Each worker tried his best to outdo the others in stretching the truth of his tales to their believable limits. Jennifer found herself caught up in the merriment surrounding her. It felt good to be unencumbered by the worries that had beset her—to laugh and enjoy the company of good friends who expected no more from her than to just be herself. All too soon the break was over, and the various workers drifted back to their respective duties.

Lingering on the steps of the building, Jennifer laughed at the story being recounted with a great deal of animation by one of the older employees, until tears rolled down her cheeks. It cheered her heart to laugh again and to realize the situation was not as gloomy as it might appear.

Despite the bitter cold weather with its thin crusts of ice on the innumerable puddles around the mill yard, the shared laugher of the two people standing on the steps made them unmindful of the chill surrounding them.

"I'm not paying you two to stand around and talk!" The voice coming from behind Jennifer and the worker was harsh with barely controlled anger.

As Jennifer spun around in surprise to face Jarrod, she was shocked by the picture he presented. He appeared to have aged beyond his years in the brief space of a few days. His eyes had lost their sparkle and fire. Lack of sleep had left its undeniable mark in the circles under dark, hollow eyes. His clothing was rumpled and seemed to hang loose over his broad frame. His stance was casual, but his shoulders appeared to have a slight droop, as if he were on the verge of suffering a great defeat and the weight was bearing on his whole countenance.

Jennifer longed to share some of the load he was bearing, to take his head in her arms and hold and comfort him. She wanted to let him know she would always be there if he ever needed or wanted her, if only he would let her into his world. No matter what had happened, she couldn't deny she cared for this man.

"Sorry, Boss, but I'm through for the day and am on my way home," answered the elderly worker, unshaken by Jarrod's abrupt tone.

The older worker refused to let his calm manner and good-natured mood be changed by the unpleasant disposition of his boss as he turned to Jennifer with a twinkle in his eye. "Don't let that overgrown kid over there give you any trouble, little lady. If he does, you just call on me anytime … day or night. I won't necessarily answer the phone … but you can call on me anyway." He winked at Jennifer and walked away without another word or even a glance in Jarrod's direction.

Jennifer smiled at the back of the departing worker and then bent to pick up her clipboard and started down the stairs.

"Where do you think you're going?" Jarrod closed the distance between them and caught her arm.

"As you said, Mr. Drake, I have work to do, and that's what you're paying me for."

"What's this *Mr. Drake* business?" Jarrod's patience was wearing thin, but Jennifer found her courage growing boulder.

"You're the boss, and I'm the employee; that is how I usually address the person in charge."

"Is that all I am to you, just the boss? I think we have a few issues to straighten out yet." Jarrod's voice softened as he turned her into his arms and captured her lips with his own.

A sob caught in her throat as she fought the struggle raging within her heart. She wanted desperately to respond to him, but too many hurts were holding her back. Was he only trying to throw her off the track and confuse her investigation of the thefts? Did he think by softening her up she would respond to his persuasions concerning God? Did she have a remote chance that he actually cared for her as a woman? No! She was not going to make a fool of herself anymore. Tears welled up in her eyes until they spilled down her cheeks.

There's no future in this, Jennifer's heart cried. She broke from his embrace and ran down the steps of the building, not conscious of the direction she headed as she raced blindly across the uneven ground of the mill yard, past the mill buildings, the open loading area, and on into the log decks. Jarrod's footsteps drew nearer as the mud began to impede her flight.

Without warning, a groan straight from the caverns of hell sounded behind Jennifer. As she turned toward the noise, her body froze with fear. Logs from the deck were picking up momentum as they rolled and tumbled over each other, heading straight for the lithe form in their pathway.

She had no place to escape the impending avalanche of timbers now threatening to bury her in a matter of seconds. Stranding transfixed, a sudden jolt from the side propelled her into the shallow water ditch surrounding the decks. The impact of a solid object forced the air from her lungs. The weight on her chest became oppressive; still she kept her eyes tightly closed, unwilling to witness her own death.

Seconds passed in slow motion as the roar of escaping logs drowned out all other sounds, and then came a stillness that eclipsed any sound.

Jennifer slowly opened her eyes, thankful to be alive. Her eyes slowly adjusted to the darkness. In the eternity of a few seconds, the solid object under which she was imprisoned began to take shape. She was shocked to see that it was not a tree trunk, as she had expected, but rather a person—Jarrod!

"Jarrod!" Jennifer searched frantically for the faintest signs of life from the body protecting her from the falling timbers. Her arms were pinned next to her sides, preventing their use in examining Jarrod to determine the extent of his injuries. The beating of her own heart was the only sign of life she could feel.

Jarrod's head lay across her shoulder, but she could not see his face. A sudden coughing sound told her he was very much alive, but it also warned her that his face was lying in the water that had, at least for now, saved their lives. If she didn't act quickly, there was a good chance he would drown. Lifting her shoulder a little allowed her to raise his face out of the water just enough for him to breathe. She had no idea how long it would be before they might be found, if at all, and it would be even longer before they were rescued. How long would it be before she was too weak to hold this position and keep Jarrod's face out of the water? How long before the icy water, already soaking through her clothing, would rob her of what little body heat she still had?

Now was not the time to panic; Jarrod's life and probably her own demanded all her strength and attention. A warm trickle of blood slid down her cheek, and though Jennifer couldn't tell where it was coming from, she guessed Jarrod must have received a head wound of some sort. She struggled to hold Jarrod's head out of the water, although he had not yet regained consciousness. The strong beat of his heart against her breast and the steady breathing next to her ear assured her she had hope at least for the time being.

Jennifer could see the daylight was fast disappearing through the jagged crevices in the logs. Soon darkness and the cold night air would set upon them with a destructive vengeance.

Fortunately for the two trapped in the ditch, the logs had not closed around them, leaving a small crawl space through the drainage ditch. Jennifer tried with all she had in her to inch her way closer to the perimeter of the log jam, but Jarrod's added weight made the task impossible. The few inches she did manage to move sorely sapped the strength from her rapidly chilling body.

Jennifer knew from her limited first-aid experience the slight shivers she was beginning to experience were the first signs of hypothermia. The logs protected them from the penetrating effects of the wind, but the icy water soaking through all of her clothing was chilling every part of her body. Her neck and shoulder muscles ached from holding Jarrod's face out of the water.

In a space of only a few minutes, the involuntary muscle spasms she was experiencing grew far more intense. Jennifer felt Jarrod also begin to shiver and realized he, too, was beginning to suffer from the cold. The only resource she had left was not within her.

"Dear God, I don't care what happens to me, but please don't let Jarrod die. He's done so much for so many people. God, I'm not going to make any promises or try to bargain with you. I know I haven't been living the way I should, but God, if You're listening to me, please, please help Jarrod." Jennifer let the warm, salty tears fall down her cheeks into the icy water that surrounded them. She hadn't given up, but she did let go, and a sweet feeling of peace soothed her mind and aching body.

A faint voice came drifting across the wind, and Jennifer listened to the silence that now encased her. She strained to catch the sound once again. Voices! She heard voices coming from somewhere above.

"We're here!" Jennifer screamed with all the strength she had in her weakened body. "Here under the logs! Please help us!"

Jarrod's weight made each attempt to fill her lungs difficult and painful. Light headiness began to overtake her, and a euphoria that nothing mattered anymore enveloped her. Laughter filled the crawl space beneath the logs. Jennifer found herself laughing at nothing and yet everything. Her mind began playing tricks as she drifted between reality and imagination.

The warmth of Jarrod's fireplace and his arms holding her firmly against his chest sent ripples of pleasure through her shivering body. Jarrod was everything Jennifer had ever dreamed a lover would be. She softly kissed his neck and whispered murmurings of love meant only for him. A brisk gust of wind wiped away the warm memories and the images that had flooded her mind. They were replaced by the stark bleakness of reality and the finality of their situation.

Was someone calling her name, or was she only imagining again? Jennifer struggled to distinguish fantasy and reality, but the cold was depriving her of her ability to reason. On the slim chance she wasn't imagining, Jennifer screamed with the last of her depleted energy.

"Jennifer? Where are you?" the voice called back.

She wasn't dreaming; someone was searching for them. "I'm here under the logs! Please help us!"

No answer! She called again, but there was still no answer. With a sigh of defeat, she allowed herself to be wrapped in the cocoon of dreams once again. The shivering had ceased, and she was no longer aware of the cold. Images of her childhood took on a haunting reality. Games she had once played with friends, both long since forgotten, were again vivid. Songs she once knew came to mind, and she gave voice to those memories of old. Even the sounds of the heavy equipment her father had once operated and would sometimes give his small daughter rides on floated through her memories.

A sudden loud cracking noise from the log jam stirred Jennifer's consciousness but not enough to bring her back to reality. A brisk blast of cold air came from somewhere above her head, but it meant nothing to Jennifer.

"Jennifer! Jennifer! Listen to me!" came a faceless voice from somewhere above her head.

"I'm okay, but I got my clothes wet. Please, Daddy, I didn't mean to ..."

"Jennifer, everything's going to be okay. Don't worry about it. We're going to slip this tether under your arms and Mr. Drake's and pull you out." The voice had a vaguely familiar face that appeared near Jennifer's head.

"Where are we going?" Jennifer asked with the delight of a small child.

"Somewhere nice and warm. Now just relax and let me do the work," the rescuer promised as he fastened the tether around the two bodies and began to pull them toward the opening created by the prongs of one of the mill's heavy equipment. The space was just high enough to provide a crawl space. One of the rescuers held her head up and made sure Jarrod's face remained above water. Their earthen shroud became further encased about them as they were pulled through the mud to safety.

Jennifer was not aware of all that occurred to either of them. Gradually she began to emerge from the fog that had closed in around her. The gentle swaying of a motor vehicle, the wail of a siren, and the coarseness of a wool blanket against her naked skin shot the final remaining mists of uncertainty from her brain.

"It's nice to see you finally decided to join the rest of us." A gentle female voice penetrated Jennifer's still drowsy senses.

"Where am I?" The memories of at least part of the last few hours came flooding back. "Where's Jarrod? Is he all right? Can I see him?" Jennifer unsuccessfully tried to escape the tight confines of the blankets that surrounded her, restoring the much-needed warmth to her cold body.

"Calm down, he's going to be fine. He's probably already at the hospital in Ukiah. They flew him out by helicopter. You can see him as soon as the doctors release you from the hospital." The attendants tried to be as gentle and reassuring as possible to alleviate their patient's distress.

The ambulance turned off the main highway and began a steep incline into the emergency entrance of the hospital.

"This isn't the Ukiah hospital!" Jennifer voiced her concern about their intended destination as she recognized some of her surroundings.

"No, this is Willits."

"I thought we were going to Ukiah. I want to see Jarrod." Jennifer's insistence bordered on hysterics.

"We have to take you to the nearest hospital, and this is it," the attendant explained patiently to Jennifer.

"Please, just take me to Jarrod."

The attendants looked at each other, unsure of how the satisfy both their patient and the state laws they were regulated by.

"I'll check with the doctor," said the driver as she exited the ambulance and entered the hospital emergency room. Within minutes she returned with the doctor, who quickly examined Jennifer's vital signs. Then he informed the ambulance personnel that she was stable enough to be transported on to Ukiah and he would sign the release. Jennifer breathed a sigh of relief as she thanked the doctor and soon drifted into a restful sleep.

Jennifer vaguely remembered voices and images, but nothing specific until she opened her eyes and watched tiny particles of matter drift lazily across the beams of sunlight shining through the slanted window blinds of her hospital room. Trying to piece the events of the previous evening together was proving more difficult than she had imagined. Thoughtfully, she ran her fingers through her hair, as if the action would help her remember what had transpired during the last few hours. Instead it brought sudden shafts of pain down her arm and across her shoulders. Her lungs and ribs ached with each breath she drew. Even the slightest muscle screamed its protest at just the thought of movement. The severe pounding in her head refused to be ignored.

She was surprised to find her hair was soft and clean. Looking at her arms and hands, she realized they were clean and fresh also. The last thing she remembered for sure was the cold, the mud, and her concern for Jarrod.

"Jarrod!" Jennifer said, voicing his name as an efficient-looking nurse entered the room and proceeded to the bedside to check on her patient's progress. "Can you tell me how Mr. Drake is?" Jennifer asked, her concern for Jarrod's wellbeing outweighing her own discomfort.

"Are you a relative, miss?" the nurse inquired.

"No, but ..."

"I'm sorry, miss, but I can't give you any information then. Maybe you could check with his doctor; he's right down the hall with Mr. Drake now."

"Thanks, I will."

Whoever said, "No news is good news" could not have known the agony of waiting for news concerning an injured loved one, Jennifer thought bitterly as a steady stream of hospital staff paraded in and out of the room, but no one offered any news of the patient just a few doors away.

Toward the noon hour, Mrs. Kent arrived with a suitcase of personal items to help make her daughter's hospital stay more comfortable.

"Hi, honey, how are you feeling?" Mrs. Kent bent to place a motherly kiss on her daughter's forehead. "Judith called me last night and told me what happened. The whole ambulance crew waited around to make sure you were okay before coming home. I do hope you didn't mind my not coming down last night to be with you, but everyone assured me there was nothing I could do." Mrs. Kent attempted to put forth a cheery disposition for the benefit of her daughter, but the puffiness and lackluster of her eyes belied her deep concern.

"That's okay, Mom, I wouldn't have known you were even here," Jennifer reassured her mother. "Have you heard anything about Jarrod?"

"I talked to Andrea this morning, and apparently he regained consciousness late last night. He has cuts and bruises, a broken shoulder blade and arm, and some cracked ribs. I stopped by his room, but they were getting ready to set his arm and put on a cast, so he wasn't there. You two were very lucky, you know."

"Yes, I—" before she could continue, the doctor arrived for his morning check on the patient.

"How are you feeling today, Miss Kent?" he asked absently, scribbling notes on the chart at the foot of the bed.

"Fine I guess, just sore," Jennifer confided.

"I'm afraid as soon as the pain medicine wears off, you're going to feel even worse."

"Thanks for that reassuring thought," Jennifer said with a groan.

"I promise you'll feel better in no time; in fact, I think it would be a good idea if you got up this evening and took a little stroll."

"How about a little ride in a wheelchair? That's more my speed right now."

The doctor chuckled as he finished his notes and hung the chart on its hook at the end of the bed. "I think a walk would be much more ... challenging."

"Did you say you graduated from med school in Transylvania?"

"Have a nice day, Miss Kent, and I'll see you later this evening." The doctor was still smiling as he nodded to the ladies and left the room.

"You look tired, dear. I think I'll check into a motel and come back a little later to see how you're doing."

"Mom, thanks, I am." Jennifer hugged her mother briefly and tried not to let her see the pain even this minor action caused. "I'm glad you're not going to try to drive all the way home again tonight."

"I may be getting older, but I'm certainly not senile yet. No way would I try to drive back home tonight and then turn around and come back again tomorrow. Now you get some rest, and I'll be back later."

Despite her desire to remain alert to try to find out something about Jarrod's condition, Jennifer found herself drifting in and out of sleep most of the day. Her first thought upon waking and the last one before drifting off again was a silent prayer for Jarrod.

The winter's sun was already drifting behind the coastal mountains as Jennifer felt the gentle coaxing of a soft female voice.

"Miss Kent, it's time to wake up. Dinner will be served in a few minutes, Miss Kent!"

Jennifer groaned as she opened her to the semi-darkness around her.

"I'm not really hungry," she replied and snuggled further under the blankets.

"Now that's what they all say, but the food isn't that bad, really." Laughter seemed to float on the air as the cheerful nurse switched on the overhead lights, flooding the room with their brightness. Jennifer winced and groaned at the pain the light caused to her eyes and head.

"As soon as you've had your dinner, Miss Kent, the doctor wants you to take a little walk."

"Now I'm sure that man is some sort of sadistic monster."

"Dr. Dawkins is one of the nicest people you'll ever meet."

"Maybe under different circumstances. Can you tell me anything about Mr. Drake? He's in the room just down the hall."

Jennifer held her breath, hoping the friendly caregiver would give her some shred of news about Jarrod's condition.

"I really don't know, miss, just that he's been in surgery most of the day and they're keeping a close watch on him."

"But I thought he had just some broken bones and stuff." Jennifer paled with alarm at the young nurse's words; her mother hadn't mentioned anything about surgery.

"I'll see what I can find out for you." She was smiling as she patted Jennifer's hand and attempted to change the subject, but her words were lost as her patient fought to control the tears clouding her eyes.

The food tray arrived and was left untouched as all Jennifer's thought and prayers focused on the room only a few doors down the hall from her own.

"Miss Kent, are you ready for that little stroll now?"

It took several second before Jennifer realized what the nurse was talking about. Without saying a word, she turned back the blankets and swung her legs over the edge of the bed. Surprise overtook her as she stared at the ugly bruises and cuts on her legs and arms. Each movement required concentration and great effort as all her muscles cried in protest at even a slight movement.

The nurse helped her into her robe and then supported her with a firm arm around her waist as they made their way out into the corridor. Each step seemed to take an eternity as the two inched their way down the long hallway. People scurried past in all directions, but Jennifer kept her eyes concentrated on the closed door halfway down the hall. The pain disappeared as each step brought her closer to her goal.

Soft organ music drifted to her ears as a set of double doors opened and closed silently. Jennifer made a mental note of the sign next to the rich oaken doors. The chapel was one place she intended to use as soon as she was able to move around on her own.

Only a few more steps and she would be there. Jennifer felt her strength ebbing away as she leaned heavily on the petite nurse.

"Maybe we should be heading back, Miss Kent. You're beginning to look a little pale again."

"No! Not yet!" Jennifer could feel droplets of perspiration forming on her forehead. Suddenly the walls began to weave, and the floor rolled like the waves of the ocean just before peaceful darkness enveloped her in its web.

Jennifer could hear voices all around her and felt the cool freshness of the sheets around her as she drifted back to reality.

"I think she'll be fine now. Maybe you were right, Miss Kent, a wheelchair would have been better." The voice resembled that of Dr. Dawkins, but she couldn't be sure.

"What happened?"

"I'm afraid you fainted on us. Now you just take it easy, and we'll try a walk again tomorrow. But let's try to eat at least a little bit before then, okay!"

Jennifer shook her head but made no attempt to speak.

"You gave us all quite a scare back there."

"I'm sorry."

"Now don't you worry about it. Just get some rest. Your mother's here; do you feel like having company?" Maybe her first impression of Dr. Dawkins had been a little inaccurate, Jennifer thought to herself as she listened to the doctor.

"Please let her come in."

Mrs. Kent's lips were smiling and cheerful as she entered her daughter's room but her eyes were dark with concern and worry.

"Heard you were trying to run away today."

Jennifer tried to laugh at her mother's lighthearted teasing but felt the stinging pain the effort caused.

"Have you heard any more about Jarrod? Why didn't you tell me he had to have surgery?"

"Now just calm down, dear. I didn't tell you about the surgery because I didn't know about it until after I left here, but from what I can gather, he's doing okay."

"Mom, please let me know as soon as you hear anything."

"Honey, you know I will. Now why don't you just try to rest? I'll just set here with my knitting for a while, if you want me to."

"I'd like that very much. Mom, please remember Jarrod in your prayers."

"Honey, you know you both are constantly in my prayers."

"Thanks, Mom." Jennifer felt her eyelids drift easily shut as she whispered a prayer for Jarrod.

Jennifer was surprised at how much better she felt the next day, and she even managed to eat whenever someone brought in a food tray.

"How do you feel about another stroll today, just a short one this time?"

"I'm really feeling much better, and we might as well get it over with," Jennifer said to the concerned nurse as she tossed back the covers. "I'll try not to cause any excitement this time."

Some of the pain and stiffness had begun to disappear as they started down the long hallway. This time they made it to Jarrod's door, and Jennifer stopped as a nurse emerged, giving her a brief glimpse into the room before the door closed.

"Why don't we see if Mr. Drake is ready for visitors yet?"

Jennifer was both surprised and delighted as she followed the young nurse into the semi-darkened room. But her hope quickly fled as she gazed upon the vacant bed.

Another attendant came into the room carrying an armload of clean linens just as the two visitors were turning to leave.

"Do you happen to know where Mr. Drake is?" the nurse asked before Jennifer had a chance to.

"I think they took him to X-ray just a little while ago, but he should be back within the hour."

"I think you should be getting back to your own room right now. Maybe we could come back this evening."

"Yes, I'd like that very much."

The rest of the day Jennifer tossed and turned, never seeming to find any peace or rest. The hours dragged by as she waited for another chance to go to Jarrod's room or at least see him, even if it was just for a few seconds.

About mid-afternoon, Jennifer threw back the covers and slid gingerly off the bed. She slowly eased her arms into the sleeves of her robe and slipped into her house slippers. Taking her time, she made her way out of the door of her room and walked unnoticed down the busy hallway toward

Jarrod's room. Pausing, she quietly pushed open the door to the hospital room.

Jarrod lay motionless on the slightly inclined bed. His normally healthy tan seemed pale in the darkened room. Jennifer was surprised at the pain that seemed etched across his handsome face. His left arm was wrapped securely in a cast and suspended in the air; a fresh gauze bandage covered most of his forehead, and the top edge of yet another cast peeked from under the sheets, contrasting sharply with the coarse, dark hair of his exposed chest.

Jennifer's heart ached at the sight of his still body lying before her so broken and hurting—all because she had been so foolish.

A low groan sent her to the side of the bed without a thought of her own pain.

"Oh, Jarrod, I'm so sorry; please forgive me."

Slowly, ever so slowly, Jarrod opened his eyes and frowned as if trying to remember something very important.

Jennifer smiled as his eyes finally settled on her and he seemed to recognize who she was.

"When are you going to get it through that thick head of yours just how dangerous it can be around the mill? I don't ever want to see you on that yard again!" Jarrod's angry words vibrated from the walls of the room.

Jennifer was shocked at his sudden outburst. The only certainty was that now she knew he not only didn't care for her but also didn't even want her around.

She turned from the bed and walked out of the room. She didn't turn around when he called her name. She was oblivious to the gasps of pain that followed her exit.

Walking almost in a trance, Jennifer made her way down the hallway and slipped into the quiet darkness of the chapel. Dropping to her knees beside one of the pews, she poured out her heart to the God she had tried to hide from for too many years. Jennifer had no idea how long she prayed and cried, but when the tears subsided, she felt a peace in her heart that had never been there before.

CHAPTER

12

"The doctor said you could go home this afternoon. Isn't that wonderful, Jennifer?" Mrs. Kent's joy illuminated her face as she began picking up her daughter's belongings and packing them into a small suitcase. As silence filled the room, she turned to face her only child. "Jennifer, is something wrong?"

"What makes you say that, Mom?"

"Oh, just little indications, like not being excited about going home, and you haven't asked me one question about Jarrod."

"Didn't I tell you I went down to see him yesterday afternoon?"

"No, you didn't. Strange, he didn't say anything about it when I stopped by to see him earlier today either. But he certainly did ask about you. He's really concerned about you."

"If you say so." Jennifer stared absently out of the window.

"Would you like me to go and see about getting you out of this place?'

"Fine." Jennifer tried to add some enthusiasm to her voice but only succeeded in sounding strained and forced.

"Dear God, please help me know what You want me to do. I can't go through this by myself," Jennifer whispered as soon as she was alone.

Jennifer was unusually quiet the next couple of days. However, everyone seemed to know she needed time to rest after her ordeal. Even Mrs. Kent didn't appear surprised by her daughter's withdrawal.

Sitting quietly on the back steps of her family home, Jennifer enjoyed the warmth of the sun as it tried to break the cold grip winter had wrapped around the valley. The trees stood barren and lonely against the stark, bleak background. Absently picking up a dry fallen leaf, she was surprised at how easily it crumbled in her hand, making only a muted crackling sound as it was torn asunder. Jennifer let the gentle breeze carry the remaining fragments across the yard. It seemed strange, but that dry, brittle leaf could just as easily have been her life these past few years, she mused, empty of life since she had turned her back on God.

Restlessly, Jennifer stood and walked across the fallen leaves that littered the yard. Leaning against the roughened trunk of a tree, she watched a trail of ants busily securing food for the long winter ahead. Events like the changing of the seasons didn't just happen. God had created all that was around her, and He was still in control. As she kicked some of the fallen leaves and watched them sail away with the wind, she was surprised to find a tiny green sprout forcing its way toward the sun among the dead and fallen leaves.

Tears came to her eyes as she knelt beside the tender young plant. Only through the death of the leaves on the tree did the new life have a chance. It could never grow strong in the shade of the mighty tree that had given it life. How like her was this delicate plant. All her life she had lived under the shadow of her dad's faith. She had never questioned, never known for herself the joy of a personal relationship with God. But when the tree was taken away, she blamed God for removing her protection, not realizing how much she needed to grow on her own. Deep within her heart, Jennifer felt the strings of joy spring to life. Even in the darkest of times she could now find hope for the future through God.

"Honey, Lieutenant Edwards is on the phone. Do you want to talk to him?" Mrs. Kent interrupted her daughter's thoughts as she called from the back door.

"Yes, Mom, I'll talk to him." To be honest, Jennifer had given little thought to her job responsibilities in the days she had been gone. It seemed a little strange, now that she thought about it, that this was the first time the lieutenant had even contacted her since the accident.

"Hello," Jennifer said cautiously into the phone, fearing Jarrod had spoken to her boss about her termination.

"Well, hello, Miss Kent. Hope you're feeling much better. Sorry I didn't get a chance to talk to you sooner, I've been out of town the last few days. I did check in at the mill for you, however, and it seems to be pretty quiet around there now that the troublemaker has been arrested. Never did trust that man!"

"I'm doing fine, thank you," Jennifer replied as soon as he paused. "And thank you also for checking on the guards for me."

"Do you have any idea how long it will be before you can go back to work?"

Jennifer breathed a sigh of relief. Apparently Jarrod had not spoken to the security company yet, giving her at least a little more time to reach some decision about the future. Jarrod had not actually said she was fired, only that *he* didn't want to see her on the yard of his mill. He would probably be in the hospital for at least another couple of weeks. Technically she could continue working until he returned.

"The doctor said maybe a week or so."

"Say, you wouldn't be interested in some other job in the company, would you?"

Jennifer's heart froze for a moment. Maybe this was the answer she had been praying for. "What other jobs are there?"

"Other places always need help, or maybe you'd be interested in a roving job where you'd only work as a fill in for a few days and then move on to another site. The head office has been talking about getting me an assistant. Maybe you'd like that job. If you're interested, why don't you let me do some checking and get back to you?"

"I'd like that very much."

"Good! Now don't you worry your pretty little head about anything. I'll see what I can do."

"Thank you again, Lieutenant. I'll be looking forward to hearing from you. Good-bye."

As she hung up the telephone, Jennifer's hope for an answer to her problem was frosted with the loneliness the future held, moving from town to town where she would always be a stranger, an outsider with no friends, leaving her mother alone most of the time ... but most of all not seeing Jarrod. It was difficult deciding what hurt the most—being near him knowing he didn't care for her the way she had come to love him or not seeing him at all.

No matter how much she prayed and tried to place her broken heart in God's keeping, the hurt was still very real.

No amount of coaxing and teasing from the mill workers could bring Jennifer out of the deep unhappiness she had entered into. Each passing day seemed even longer than the previous one.

Everywhere she turned, she found reminders of Jarrod Drake, from the giant letters across the front of the three-story mill to the signs painted neatly on every vehicle on the yard. She could not escape his presence.

The florescent lights of the mill's interior whispered a gentle hum as they stood guard over the silent powerful saws, and endless rollers and miles of chain invoked a feeling that the inner workings of the mill had a presence and will of their own. They could effortlessly spring to life at any moment and devour the unsuspecting.

The fleeting memory of Jarrod's sleeping form flashed before the solitary figure as she stood and silently gazed at the massive machinery around her. He, too, exuded the same feelings. The gentle breathing that concealed a powerful being but with a difference; Jarrod cared! He really cared and tried to help those in need. Jennifer stopped suddenly. Maybe what she had taken as feelings of love from him was only his concern for her spiritual well-being.

Jennifer felt her heart contract as she realized the depth of Jarrod's faith in God. If only she could come to know even a fraction of the faith he had, maybe the peace and happiness she had been searching for would finally be hers.

Even the weather offered Jennifer no relief from the constant assault on her senses by Jarrod's memory. The harsh, bitter downpours that soaked through any protective clothing to chill her body to its very core spoke of his final orders at the hospital that had wounded her heart so deeply.

The gentle raindrops and mist caressed her checks as softly and tenderly as the touch of his hand or lips against her skin.

"Jennifer, phone call for you," yelled one of the guards from the steps of the small lunchroom building.

"Who is it?" Jennifer asked, hoping it wasn't Jarrod.

"Sounds like Lieutenant Edwards," replied the other guard.

Breathing a sigh of relief, Jennifer walked to the telephone and picked up the receiver. "Hello."

"Jennifer, this is Lieutenant Edwards. I may have some good news for you. Talked to the head office today, and they like the idea of you working as a fill in at all our job sites. They would like to meet you and work out some of the minor details if that would be agreeable with you?"

"That sounds fine. When do they want to have the meeting?"

"Well, it will probably be the first of next week before everyone can get together. How does Tuesday sound? I'll be by about 8:30 to pick you up." Without giving Jennifer a chance to answer, the lieutenant ended the conversation.

Even the prospect of another job did little to lift her sagging spirits as she replaced the receiver back into its cradle.

From the rumors circulating the mill, Jennifer gathered that Jarrod's physical condition was improving, but apparently he hadn't yet recovered his easygoing disposition, and this concerned many who knew him. Time was beginning to run out for Jennifer.

The small gathering of nightshift workers made their way across the yard and entered the small wooden structure that served as their lunchroom and locker area. Most of the conversations on this particular evening were serious due to all the events that had occurred in such a short span of time. Jennifer listened disinterestedly for a few minutes while she finished the last of her reports and slipped unnoticed out into the stillness of the calm winter night.

A couple of jackrabbits watched the unhurried pace of the young woman before they scampered across her path and headed toward the tall grasses of the sloping hillsides surrounding the flat mill yard. The high-pitched cry of the killdeers broke the silence of the darkness as they hurried away from the human intruder before taking flight.

A warm smile crossed her face as Jennifer watched the wild creatures she had come to appreciate and admire in the short time she had been allowed the privilege of observing the many beautiful animals co-habiting the mill yard with the human populace. They lived in constant danger with their choice of residence but still managed to adapt themselves readily to the continual changes taking place around them.

Of course, causalities did occasionally occur, but in comparison to the general wildlife community, not enough to make any significant difference. Jennifer remembered the Sunday school stories she had heard while growing up about all the hurting and broken people Jesus had healed while He was here on earth. Maybe she was one of the human causalities that only God could heal.

She had come to love and respect so many characteristics about this place—the rich, fragrant aroma of the up-turned earth after a rain storm or when the sun had dried and parched it and allowed the wind to transport fine particles of dust and bark to other corners of the valley.

She always felt a strong sense of pride as she watched the loads of logs being trucked into the yard, unloaded, and stacked with expert accuracy in the tall decks to await their turn to be processed. She still experienced fascination and awe whenever she watched the logs being transformed into the finished boards they would become. The beauty of the fresh-cut slabs of wood and fresh, pungent perfume that always drifted across the wind to stir her emotions with awareness of the wonderful beauty around her.

She would always remember the new friends she had come to know and love here at the mill and the volumes of new information that had been opened to her from the very first day she had set foot on the property.

This was not just a job to her anymore, to be completed in the eight hours of her shift and then to be forgotten until the next day. This place and everything about it had become a part of her life. It was a part she was going to miss very much when she left. The mill was an exciting new world she had come to love—Jarrod's world.

That thought brought a return of the sadness she had struggled with over the past several days. Jennifer stopped to watch a tiny frog as it leaped from one small puddle to another.

Glancing around, she could see several areas where the guards had helped bring about improvements at the mill, whether it was a new light as some dark corner of the yard or a bulldozer path along the fence line. They may not have been improvements that others were likely to notice, but she knew they were there. Like the tiny frog whose presence would go virtually unnoticed, her influence, too, would eventually fade away, but she knew that she had been there and the memories and emotions gathered from this place would be with her the rest of her life.

This would probably be her last chance to imprint all the sights and feelings she wanted to remember, she reluctantly mused as she prolonged her self-guided tour as long as possible.

The main office area was locked, but for some time, she stood in the shadow of the giant oak trees that shaded the building from the direct rays of the sun. She saw images of Jarrod poring over some report or problem at the spacious desk or reclining casually, gazing out the vast glass wall behind his chair, watching the activities of his domain. She relived the excitement and thrill she experienced whenever he had shared some small recollection or asked her opinion concerning some article he had just finished reading ... Then, unheeded, she remembered the embarrassment she always felt as she tried to read and discuss with some degree of intelligence the material, always under the intimidation of his steady gaze. With a heavy sigh, Jennifer turned away from the well-lit building and made her way back across the yard one last time.

So far everyone had honored her unspoken request for privacy, so Jennifer was caught off guard when Andrea not only invaded this restricted area but seemed determined to find out what was going on when the two women met by accident at the small community post office the following day.

"Why haven't you been to see Jarrod or at least called him?" Andrea demanded.

"I don't think that's any of your business," Jennifer replied, sharper than she had intended.

"Well, I'm making it my business! Listen, Jennifer, we've been friends a long time, and I only want to help," Andrea continued, undaunted by Jennifer's obvious reluctance to discuss the matter. "He asks about you every day, you know."

"You didn't tell him I'm still working at the mill, did you?"

"Of course, why shouldn't I?" Andrea looked surprised that Jennifer would even have asked such a question.

"Because the last statement he said to me at the hospital was that he never wanted to see me on the mill yard again." Jennifer felt sharp pains of hurt and regret pierce her heart as she recalled the sharpness in Jarrod's voice.

"I'm sure he didn't mean you were fired. He cares for you very much and doesn't want anything to happen to you."

"I wish I could believe you," Jennifer answered sadly.

"Jennifer, why don't you talk to him? I'm sure this is just a little misunderstanding between you two and can easily be straightened out. Please go and see him," Andrea pleaded as she watched the emotional turmoil Jennifer was experiencing cloud her translucent blue eyes.

"Thank you for your concern, Andrea, but I'm afraid it's too late." Jennifer's voice was void of emotion as she turned to go.

Andrea caught her arm. "It's not too late to tell him you love him, and I think you do."

"And make a fool of myself."

"You'd rather spend the rest of your life being miserable just because you *might* make a fool of yourself? I really can't believe how much alike you two are. I certainly hope that one of you makes up your mind soon." Andrea's irritation grew with each word she spoke.

"I've already made up my mind," replied Jennifer with calmness in her voice that belied her inner turmoil. "I have an appointment in Eureka with the district managers next week about a transfer."

Andrea was speechless at Jennifer's announcement and stared wide eyes in disbelief at the younger girl. Seizing the momentary lull in the discussion, Jennifer quickly escaped the confines of the small public building and Andrea's prying questions.

The Kent house was quiet when Jennifer finally made her way home from the post office and her encounter with Andrea. Often in the past, she had been able to receive a temporary reprieve from her problems in the balm of a nice hot bath. After a brief search of the bathroom closets, she located a small bottle of bubble bath.

After pouring most of the contents of the container under the faucet, she watched the transformation of the steaming clear water into a billowing cloud of soft white bubbles. After pinning her hair into a loose twist on the top of her head, she slipped gingerly into the torrid water-and-oil mixture, easing herself under its fragrant ensconce.

Time seemed to stand still as she lay under the warm cover of water and bubbles, enjoying the luxury of her tranquil surroundings, but the persistent ring of the telephone threatened to disturb her peace. She chose to ignore its existence for several rings but finally changed her mind and grabbed a towel. She wrapped it securely around her wet, soft skin as she dashed out the bathroom door and down the stairs, leaving a trail of soapy footprints along her bath.

"Hello?" Jennifer questioned, her voice soft and breathy from the brief sprint to reach the offending instrument. The only response was the impersonal buzz of a disconnected call. Maybe one of these days the modern world would catch up with this part of the country, Jennifer thought as she replaced the receiver and wished that at least caller ID would soon be available in the valley.

Retracing her steps, she used the free end of the towel to wipe away her soapy footprints. Slight chills ran over her uncovered flesh as she made her way along the upstairs hall. Memories of the bitter cold she had experienced when she was pinned under the escaping logs just a few short days earlier ran through her mind and only increased her trembling.

Retrieving her warm cold weather robe from the closet, Jennifer sat for a long time on the edge of the bed that had occupied her room from her earliest memories. Clutching her forearms as if to protect herself, Jennifer gently rocked back and forth, remembering the many happy times she had spent in the protective shelter of this small room. Opening the drawer of the nightstand, she took out a well-worn Bible and reverently opened its pages. For several minutes Jennifer read random passages that seemed to take on new meanings as she now read them with more understanding. Quietly she whispered a prayer, asking God to come into her heart and become as real to her as He had been to both her dad and Jarrod.

Tiny, sparkling tears slipped silently down her pale cheeks to fall unnoticed into the fabric of her robe. Finally complying with the wishes of her heart, she softly cried herself into a restful repose.

A distant bell rang, but its high-pitched voice was quickly hushed as Jennifer stirred briefly form her slumber. The door to her room opened, and the soft, gentle hand of her mother rested on her shoulder.

"Jennifer, you have a phone call." Mrs. Kent's voice was kind but firm in its announcement.

"Who is it?" Jennifer asked as she rubbed some of the sleep from her face.

"Sounds like your boss."

"Lieutenant Edwards—wonder what he wants?" Jennifer questioned irritably as she swept past her mother and made her way to the phone.

"Yes," came her abrupt greeting to the party on the other end of the line.

"Miss Kent, I hate to bother you at this late hour, but Eureka just called and they want to see us first thing tomorrow morning. Can you leave either later this evening or very early tomorrow morning, say around 4:00 a.m.?"

"This is short notice, Lieutenant ... maybe I should just meet you at Highway 101 tomorrow morning."

"You sure you don't want to go up tonight?"

"No, that's fine. I'd just as soon go up tomorrow. Thank you for asking anyway."

"Okay, Miss Kent, guess I'll see you bright and early in the morning then. Better get some rest."

"Good-bye, Lieutenant."

A deep frown creased Jennifer's brow as she replaced the telephone.

"Is there something wrong, dear? You look a little worried. I thought tomorrow was your day off. Are you planning on going somewhere?" Mrs. Kent questioned her daughter with caution.

"Everything's just fine, Mom. I have to go to a meeting tomorrow in Eureka with Lieutenant Edwards, nothing to worry about." Now was not the time to mention her possible relocation so soon after the accident, Jennifer reasoned, as she tried to act as if the trip was merely a routine matter.

CHAPTER

13

Jennifer glanced at her watch for the third time within the last five minutes and tried to remain calm. It had been hard enough to drag herself out of bed in the middle of the night and then to drive the twisting Covelo Road, only to be kept waiting in the cold darkness for almost forty-five minutes. It was almost unforgivable.

The damp chill of the night seemed to creep through her clothing enough to cause shivers to run up and down her limbs. The black wool slacks and bulky gray sweater were nice enough, but certainly nothing special, which matched the occasion perfectly. The black high-topped boots and very light makeup completed the casualness of her attire.

Jennifer swayed between irritation and concern for her boss's tardiness as she glanced once again at her watch. She stared intently down the bleak stretch of highway, as though this action alone would produce the lieutenant. Jennifer was both surprised and relieved as the small economy car, supplied by the security company, finally rounded the corner and began slowing down as it came closer.

"Sorry I'm late ... had some car trouble," volunteered the tardy officer without any further comment. He motioned for Jennifer to get into the passenger's seat of the car.

"Would you like to take my car then?" Jennifer suggested, a bit concerned about the reliability of the company car.

"No, think everything is fine now, but we'd better get going if we're going to make it on time."

Glancing at her watch again, Jennifer mentally calculated how fast they would have to travel to finish the trip on time. She doubted they would arrive at the appointed hour.

The canopy of sinister dark clouds only added to the gloom that had besieged her from the moment the lieutenant had proposed this trip. Today she saw no sunshine on the crested hills. No soft, mellow symphonies drifted about the interior of the car as she had enjoyed on her previous trip to salve her confused and battered emotions. Besides the gloom of the weather, the miserly padding of the seats in the inexpensive automobile offered little protection against the impact of the potholes and rocks on the roadway for its passengers.

She heard only the clattering noises of the stingy engine of the car as it strained to pull even the slightest incline. The contrast between this trip and the one she had taken with Jarrod was overwhelming.

Despite the cold, rainy weather, Jennifer was forced to open her window in order to allow fresh air to circulate the close quarters of the automobile. The incessant chain smoking of her boss irritated both her eyes and disposition.

"I never did find out why you were even interested in a transfer." Lieutenant Edwards's question startled Jennifer out of her deep contemplation.

"I don't recall you ever asked why, but I just feel it's time for a change of scenery." Jennifer spoke with very little enthusiasm in her voice.

"You and the almighty Mr. Drake didn't get into a fight or something, did you? You two seemed pretty chummy at the owner's meeting. That kind of thing usually leads to trouble sooner or later, if you know what I mean." A slight sneer curled the corners of his thick lips as he spoke Jarrod's name.

"Mr. Drake had nothing to do with my decision, and we do not have, nor did we ever have, anything going on between us." Jennifer snapped the harsh words at her antagonist more out of regret than defense.

The countryside passed quickly as the car sped over the ribbon of asphalt winding alongside the mighty Eel River. The recent rains had swollen the once-peaceful river into a torrent of churning white water and debris rushing past on its way to the ocean.

The image of a dark-haired young man risking his own safety to help others who were less fortunate permeated Jennifer's thoughts as she gazed at the temperamental river. Jarrod was always looking out for the welfare and safety of others. If she hadn't been so stubborn, he would not be lying in the hospital right now.

A chill trembled through her body as she remembered the icy water and muddy covering that had almost become their tomb.

The driver mistook her shiver as being cold. "If you'd close that window, you wouldn't be so cold."

"Then I wouldn't be able to breathe." Jennifer tried to soften the hostility in her tone of voice but without much success.

"I forgot you don't smoke." The words were spoken offhandedly, as the driver took another puff on his cigarette.

Jennifer didn't even bother replying to his comment as she stared out the car window and the changing terrain from the forested hills to rolling inland coastal valleys, dotted with small clusters of farms houses surrounded by grazing herds of sheep and cattle.

Jennifer breathed a sigh of relief when they at last pulled into the parking lot of a small office complex. The pungent order of the area fisheries immediately assaulted them as they walked toward the building.

The office was sparse but efficient, and a pleasant middle-aged secretary greeted them as soon as they opened the door. Lieutenant Edwards made a brief introduction and stated their business to the somewhat-surprised office worker.

"I'm sorry, Lieutenant Edwards, but Mister Gradden is not going to be in the office today, and he said nothing to me about having a meeting this morning."

"But I just talked to him yesterday, and he told me to come up on Friday, and that's today."

"I'm sorry, but today is Thursday; I do see that you are on the calendar for tomorrow morning at 9:00."

"Now what are we supposed to do?" Jennifer clutched her fists tightly as she spoke, her growing anger making each word an effort to utter.

"Well, unless you want to come back up again tomorrow morning, I suggest we just get motel rooms for the night."

"But I didn't come prepared to stay overnight."

"You could always go buy the stuff you have to have ... you've got all day. I'm going to see about getting the car fixed." Walking out the door as he spoke, the older man left Jennifer standing in the middle of the room, stunned.

Turning briskly on her heels, Jennifer followed her employer out to the parking lot, slamming the door behind her.

"What kind of game are you playing here?" Jennifer grabbed at the lieutenant's arm and spun him around to face her.

"I'm not the one who's playing games, Missy. And don't you pull that innocent school girl routine on me. I know your kind ... think you're too good to be with someone like me!"

"Just what are you talking about?"

"Never mind, get in the car and I'll take you to the shopping mall so you can pick up the stuff you need while I get the car worked on."

The silence in the car was thick as the driver maneuvered in and out of the traffic, finally pulling into the spacious shopping center.

"I'll meet you here about four o'clock. That should give you plenty of time to shop," Edwards stated as he pulled next to the curb.

Glancing at her watch, Jennifer shook her head in agreement, climbed out of the car, and walked toward one of the stores without looking back.

Her first stop once inside the shopping complex was a public telephone; she searched the directory for Bradley's lumber company.

"Redwood Empire, may I help you?"

"Yes, I'd like to speak to Bradley, please."

"I'm sorry, but Mister Evans is in a meeting and cannot be disturbed. May I take a message?"

"Just tell him Jennifer Kent called and I'll try back later this afternoon. Thank you for your help."

Disappointed at not being able to speak to Bradley, Jennifer leisurely began making her way through the stores, surprised at how quickly the time was passing. After purchasing the few items she needed for the night, she began to make her way back to the rendezvous point. She was more than a little surprised to find the car waiting for her and the lieutenant in an unusually pleasant mood.

"Would you like dinner before we check in at the motel?" As he held open the passenger door, he seemed to be trying very hard to make amends for his earlier behavior.

"I'm not really hungry."

"I know a little place right up the road here where the food is real good. We really should eat something." This time Edwards was more persistent as he maneuvered the car through the late-afternoon traffic.

Ignoring her displeasure at his suggestion for dinner, the driver parked the car in front of a small group of older buildings in the lower-rent district of the city.

Taking her time gathering her purse and coat before she exited the car, Jennifer finally joined her companion on the sidewalk. This time Edwards made no attempt to extend even the simplest gentlemanly manners toward his passenger and lit another cigarette as he waited impatiently for her to join him.

The café was not much more than a hole-in-the-wall establishment with only a few mismatched tables and chairs filling the room. A counter with backless stools skirted one wall, broken only by a set of swinging doors into what appeared to be the kitchen area. A few customers were scattered around the room, and no one seemed to notice them as they stood for a moment in the doorway. The interior was old and shabby. If anything could be called a greasy spoon café, this was it. Jennifer lost any semblance of an appetite as the lieutenant chose a table for them toward the back of the room.

Edwards had already seated himself and was glancing over the menu as Jennifer dusted the crumbs off her chair before sitting down.

Noticing her actions and distasteful glance around the establishment, her companion retorted sharply, "This may not be as fancy as Mister Rich Boy might take you to, but it will do just fine for tonight."

Jennifer stiffened at his insulting reference to Jarrod.

"Listen, honey, you'll soon learn that one man will do just as well as the next, so you'd better get use't to it." Lieutenant Edwards didn't even bother to look at Jennifer as he continued scanning the menu.

Soft drinks were served in cans and appeared to be the only item on the menu that might be sanitary enough to consume. Having made her choice, Jennifer waited quietly until it arrived, requested a straw, and then slowly sipped the cold liquid, avoiding all attempts at conversation from her dinner companion.

After his dinner arrived, he, too, made no further attempts to converse with her, more interested in the food and large amount of beer he was consuming than in the young woman with him.

When he finally finished his meal, the lieutenant rose from the table, never asking Jennifer if she were ready to leave. As they made their way to the cashier, Edwards stumbled in his inebriated condition but refused any assistance.

The cool night air helped revive the man enough that he felt capable of operating the car the few remaining blocks to the motel, despite protests from Jennifer as to his fitness for driving. She did not appreciate the position or danger in which he had put both of them by insisting on driving in his present state of intoxication. He refused to listen to any of her pleas or arguments, and she only succeeded in making him more determined and angrier than he had previously been.

Jennifer remained alert and on guard for any possible problems as they traversed the remaining distance to their destination, silently praying to God for His protection every inch of the way.

She was very much relieved as they pulled up to the office of a budget motel complex. The lieutenant instructed Jennifer to remain in the car while he completed the transaction for their stay.

When he returned to the car, he handed Jennifer the key to her room and quickly put his own key, along with another smaller object, into his pocket and drove to the back of the two-story building.

Jennifer was thankful she had only a few items with her as they climbed the open stairs to their second-story rooms. Edwards made a brief muttered comment about having an errand to run as they stepped onto the landing outside their respective rooms and that he would return in a little while.

Jennifer was relieved that at least for a short time she would not have to endure his company. The air was stale as Jennifer felt the wall for the light switch. She was not surprised by the Spartan atmosphere of the room, but at least it offered the privacy and rest she sorely needed.

Sitting wearily on the edge of the bed, she reached for the telephone to call her mother and let her know of the change of plans.

"Mom, I'll be fine. Don't worry, okay? I'll be home tomorrow." Jennifer did her best to sound casual and relaxed but could tell by her mother's voice that her portrayal was not very convincing.

"Honey, Jarrod called today."

"What did you tell him?" Jennifer felt the muscles across her shoulders tighten as she waited for a response.

"I just told him you went to Eureka for a meeting. Why, do you have something you need to tell him?"

"What makes you say that?"

"Nothing in particular and a lot of things in general, like why you're avoiding him. You haven't even tried to find out how he's doing."

"Are you sure it's not just your imagination? I know exactly how he's doing; that's all they talk about out at the mill. Now I'm fine, and I'll be home tomorrow sometime. I love you Mom."

"I love you too, honey, and I'll be praying for you that you'll find an answer for whatever it is that's troubling you."

"Thanks, Mom. Good night."

Pausing momentarily before she hung up the receiver, Jennifer whispered a silent prayer of her own for the loving parents God had provided her and for Jarrod's recovery.

After picking up the local telephone directory, she decided to make one more phone call before turning in for the night. She glanced at her watch and hesitated, almost certain no one would be there to answer her call.

The other end of the line began to ring as she counted each resonant sound echoing in her ear; seven ... eight ... nine.

"Redwood Empire, Bradley Evans."

The clear, deep voice sounded like music straight from heaven to Jennifer's ears.

"Bradley! I'm so glad I caught you."

"Jennifer! I wish my secretary had told me you were on the phone when you called earlier. How are you?"

"Oh, I'm doing okay. In fact, I'm here in town tonight."

"That's great. I wish I had known sooner you were coming up. Maybe we could have had dinner together. Unfortunately, now I have a meeting to attend this evening."

"Thank you, but I didn't mean to put you on the spot. I just wanted to touch base and see how you were, that's all."

"Oh, I'm great. But what I want to know is what's going on with you and that old rascal of a buddy of mine. I can't get any news out of him."

"Well, one of the reasons may be because we have nothing going on between us."

"If that's how you want to play, okay. But I'd better be the first to know when you two make up your minds. Say, listen, let me give you my home phone number just in case you need anything."

Jennifer quickly scribbled the number on a piece of paper and thanked Bradley for his friendship before saying good-bye.

After hanging up the phone, she decided it would be a good time to shower and wash her hair to remove as much of Edward's tobacco odor as possible.

After discarding her clothes and grabbing a couple of towels, she headed for the outdated shower stall in the corner alcove of the room. The sting of hot water pelting against her soft skin at last began to ease some of the tension that had been building up most of the day.

She had experienced other trying times in her life, and she had always been able to see her way through. Now she knew without a doubt that God was indeed with her and would guide her every step of the way. In time, her hurting would begin to ease, and with His help, she would someday be happy. For now all she needed or wanted was to sleep and for a short while at least, be free of the turmoil she was experiencing.

After wrapping a towel around her wet hair, she slipped into the new gown she had purchased at the mall and curled up on the bed to rest just a little while before drying her thick hair and turning in for the night.

She picked up the well-worn Bible on the nightstand and let the pages fall where they may as the book opened to reveal God's Word. She was pleased and surprised to find herself reading the story of Daniel and the lion's den. Somewhere in the story, sleep overcame the reader, and she drifted into a peaceful slumber.

The sound of a key turning in a lock suddenly awakened the startled sleeper. The door connecting her room to that of Lieutenant Edwards slowly began to open.

Scrambling to her feet, Jennifer grabbed the first loose object within her reach. The bed separated her from the intruder and offered a small degree of protection for the moment.

The strong stench of liquor preceded the unwanted visitor as he stumbled into the room. His clothes were in a sad state of disarray as the lieutenant made his way further into the dimly lit room.

"What do you want?" Jennifer demanded defiantly.

"Now come on, little lady, you'd just better start learning to nicer to people." His speech was thick and slurred as he continued his slow progression in Jennifer's direction.

"Get out of here!" Jennifer shouted, the danger she was in growing more apparent with each passing second.

"Bet you didn't play this tough with Old Drake to get those stripes."

"What do you mean by that?" His statement took her completely by surprise.

"Don't play that innocent game with me. You know he told the company if you weren't put in charge up there they could pull everyone out. And Glen and me had plans for that place, too. We could have stolen Mr. High and Mighty blind, till you messed everything up."

Jennifer's head was swimming with the implications of everything the drunken man was saying.

"You! You were the one driving the truck when Glen was caught! You must have set the fire too!" Jennifer yelled at the intruder, shocked by her new discoveries.

"A lot of good it's going to do you, missy. You can't prove nothing!"

Stunned by the revelations, Jennifer failed to notice Lieutenant Edwards had advanced closer across the room until it was too late. His hand snaked out to ensnare her arm. Fighting to keep her balance, she quickly turned. Before he knew what was taking place, she managed to execute the same type of shoulder throw that had catapulted Jarrod to the ground.

Edwards left a trail of destruction as he fell, knocking over several pieces of furniture and breaking a table lamp before coming to rest near the front door of the room.

As he attempted to get to his feet, Jennifer opened the door to the room, and pushed with all her might, propelling the out-of-shape man onto the motel's catwalk railing.

She quickly closed and locked the door, ran, and closed the connecting entrance to the adjoining room, securing it as best she could with a chair. Getting away from this room and Edwards were the only thoughts that pounded in her head.

Hurriedly, Jennifer began collecting what few belongings she had. She called the front desk, requested a taxi, and then sat in the darkened room listening for any sounds from Edwards, alternately praying for God's protection and thanking Him for what He had already done.

The shrill ring of the phone caused her to jump with a start as she hesitantly picked up the receiver. She was relieved to hear the night manager calling to inform her the taxi she ordered had arrived.

Opening the outside door cautiously, Jennifer checked for any sign of Edwards, just in case she had failed to notice his return. The walkway was vacant as she exited the disheveled room and almost ran down the staircase to the waiting taxi, leaving the events of the last few hours disappearing into the thickening coastal fog.

CHAPTER

14

"Where to, miss?"

The cab driver seemed extremely polite as he began to maneuver the automobile through the parking lot.

Seeking an answer to his question, Jennifer realized she had no place to go and no idea who to turn to. "I'm not sure."

"How about a little hint?"

"I only know one person here, and I don't know where he lives."

"Want to give him a call and get directions? I see a phone booth right over there."

Jennifer smiled her appreciation as the driver pulled up next to the curb.

Clutching the scrap of paper she had scribbled on, Jennifer tried the number several times with no success.

Discouraged, she returned to the back seat of the cab, very close to tears, the events of the evening taking their toll.

"Listen, miss, who is this friend of yours? I've lived here all my life and sure know a lot of people. Wouldn't hurt to give it a try." His sincerity was genuine, and Jennifer marveled at his concern after years of dealing with the disinterested cabbies of San Francisco.

"Evans, Bradley Evans. Do you know him?" A glimmer of hope sparked on the bleak horizon.

A broad smile flashed across the cabby's face as he turned and quickly pulled the car into the traffic.

"Sure, I know Bradley. He goes to my church, and I know right where he lives. It's really a nice place too. I understand he built it all himself."

Jennifer leaned her head against the window and watched the lights of the city float in and out of the fog. Gone were the doubts and questions. God was real! Like the stories in the Bible, He provided for His own. Tears slipped down her checks as she thought of all the time she had wasted trying to do things her own way. Jarrod had been right when he had told her that until she accepted God on His terms and not her own, she would never find peace.

"Thank You, God, for sending Jarrod into my life. I'm afraid without his help I might never have found the way back to where I belong." The words were spoken silently, but the depth of emotions they expressed was shouted from the highest mountaintop to the heavens above.

"Well, here we are, miss. Are you all right?"

"I'm fine, thank you. In fact, I'm feeling better than I have ever been in my life," Jennifer reassured the cabby, smiling tranquilly as tears glistened down her cheeks.

Lights of an approaching car flooded the interior of the cab and quickly darkened as the vehicle parked behind them.

"Looks like perfect timing," the driver stated as he slid out of the car and opened the door for his passenger. "Hi, Bradley, got a guest for you."

"Jennifer!" Bradley seemed truly surprised to see this particular guest. "This is a surprise."

"I hope this is not inconvenient for you." Jennifer was almost afraid to look into Bradley's face as she spoke.

"You know it's not." Bradley gently lifted her chin and studied her tear-stained face. "Is everything all right?"

"Oh, Bradley!" Jennifer circled her arms around her host's waist and released the stream of tears welled up inside her, tears of joy, tears of fear and anger, tears of extreme fatigue.

"Come on inside. I've got a mighty big shoulder you can cry on. How much do I owe you, Henry?"

"This one's on me, Brad. I'll keep you both in my prayers tonight, buddy."

"Thanks." Bradley gently guided Jennifer toward the large wooden entry way to the house. A soft whining sound penetrated the quietness of the night.

"That's just Samson. You'll meet him in a minute," Bradley assured Jennifer as he turned the key in the locked door and pushed it open, much to the joy of the huge golden lab that bounded immediately toward his owner. Bending slightly, Bradley played affectionately with the animal before releasing him to run in the front yard.

"He's beautiful," Jennifer said with a slight smile.

"Thanks, but let's get inside and you tell me what's wrong." After directing Jennifer into the living room, Bradley turned and with a sharp whistle brought Samson running back into the house, instantly at the heels of his master. "That's a good boy. Now I want you to be on your best behavior, boy, because I want to introduce you to someone very special."

The animal's ears perked up as he watched Bradley's every move. He tagged along dutifully at his master's side and sat patiently when Bradley stopped in front of Jennifer.

"Samson, I'd like you to meet Jennifer Kent. Jennifer, this is Samson." Bradley smiled as he made the formal introductions.

"I'm very pleased to meet you, Samson," Jennifer responded, extending her hand to pet the well-mannered animal. She couldn't help but laugh as a large, damp paw landed in the palm of her outstretched hand.

"I'd say you meet with his approval," Bradley laughingly assured Jennifer as he scratched Samson's large head. "How about some hot chocolate? I'd offer coffee, but I'm afraid you'd have to drink it by yourself. It'd keep me awake all night if I had some this late."

"Hot chocolate would be fine."

Jennifer followed Bradley into the small kitchen area as he began collecting the ingredients for their drinks.

"Bradley, I'm sorry for imposing on you like this, especially so late, but I really didn't know where else to go or what to do."

"Well, why don't you just tell me what's wrong, and we'll take it from there?"

"I'm not sure where to begin," Jennifer answered honestly as she settled on one of the stools along the eating counter of the kitchen.

"I'll tell you what, let me get a fire going in the fireplace while you watch the milk on the stove and collect your thoughts, and we'll sit down in the living room and talk."

Jennifer was grateful for the extra time to sort out her thoughts. After mixing the milk and cocoa, she filled their cups and dropped in some of the marshmallows Bradley had found. A fire was blazing in the natural stone fireplace that dominated one wall of the room. Well-stocked bookshelves on both sides made it the focal point of the room. The dancing flames reflected off the gleaming surface of the aged hardwood floors, covered only sparsely with braided rugs. A rich leather recliner, positioned comfortably a few feet from the fireplace, spoke of many a long evening of relaxing for the person lucky enough to enjoy it.

Jennifer found the large, overstuffed couch much to her liking as Bradley encouraged her to make herself comfortable, opting for a pillow on the hearth rather than a chair for himself. Samson leisurely stretched himself out on the rug in front of the warming fire, paying little attention to the humans who were now sharing his domain.

"I guess I should start at the beginning," Jennifer said thoughtfully.

"That sounds like a good place," Bradley teased lightly.

Reflecting the leisurely pace of her surroundings, Jennifer began telling about her childhood experiences in church and her arguments with her father that finally caused her to run away from the valley. She told him of her return home, including the near accident with Jarrod. She explained how Jarrod had helped her come to terms with a personal experience with God and how she had misinterpreted his actions to mean more than he had intended. She told him about the accident and how Jarrod had saved her life and about Jarrod telling her he never wanted to see her on his mill yard again. Jennifer then related the incident earlier in the evening with Lieutenant Edwards.

She was surprised when she paused and heard the grandfather clock in the corner of the room striking. Glancing at her watch to make sure she had heard the right number of chimes, she discovered the time had quickly slipped away and it was now well into the wee hours of the morning, and the once-blazing fire was but a bed of glowing embers.

"Bradley, why didn't you tell me it was so late?"

"Because it was important for you to get all your emotions entirely out in the open and not keep them bottled up inside. Some of the things you've told me I'm going to have to look into, but I have a feeling everything's going to work out for the best. I think what you need right now is a good night's rest. Why don't you take the guest room down the hall and we'll talk again tomorrow."

"Thanks for being such a good listener."

"My pleasure." Bradley gently kissed her on the forehead and then turned her in the direction of the guest room. "Now you get some sleep, and that's an order."

Jennifer gave a snappy salute as she marched down the hall and through the door Bradley had indicated would be her room for the evening.

"There's a bathroom through the door on the left. If you need anything, just holler. Good night, Jennifer."

"Good night, Bradley, and thanks for everything." Jennifer smiled sweetly as she closed the door.

It seemed like only a few seconds had passed since Jennifer had snuggled down under the covers of the large four-poster bed and closed her eyes, suddenly realizing how tired she really was.

Small particles danced in the shafts of golden sun that streamed through the slits of the blinds on the bedroom windows. The house was quiet except for the ticking of the ancient clock down the hall. Jennifer stretched leisurely before throwing back the covers and heading for the shower. The hot water and fresh-smelling soap washed away all the filth and grime she felt still clinging to her after the incident of the previous evening.

Wrapped in the large bath towel she found in the bathroom, Jennifer looked at her meager choice of clothing. She tried to wipe any dirt spots or wrinkles out of the fabric before she slipped once again into the outfit she had worn for two days now. She wrinkled her nose in disgust at the stale tobacco odor that still clung to the material.

When she walked out of the guest room and down the hall of the house, she was pleased at the warm, inviting feeling that surrounded her. The house was small, but she did not feel cramped in its close quarters, only secure. The dark wood of the floor was offset by cream-colored walls with dark wood trim. The rooms were full but not cluttered, giving the place a comfortable, lived-in look.

A scratching noise followed by a soft whining sound directed Jennifer's attention to the French doors off the main room of the house. There sat Samson, not so patiently waiting for someone to let him in the house.

"Good morning, boy, where's you master today?" Jennifer scratched the dog's head in the same manner she had seen Bradley doing.

Glancing past the dog, Jennifer was delighted by what she found. The house was perched on a small cliff overlooking a long, beautiful beach that stretched for what seemed like miles to the south but was interrupted a short distance to the north by sheer cliffs rising abruptly from the floor of the ocean. The floor-to-ceiling windows allowed unobstructed views in several directions. The blue skies merged far on the horizon with the grayish-blue of the Pacific Ocean. Seagulls circled and then swooped sharply as they searched for their morning's meal. The ceaseless roll of the waves crashed onto the beach and then crept back to try once again.

Jennifer breathed in the fresh salt air and vowed to explore the beach as soon as she could. Wandering back into the house, she spotted a large piece of paper propped against a beautifully refurbished roll-top desk.

Jennifer,

Sorry I wasn't here when you got up this morning but something has come up and I had to go out of town. Please make yourself at home. You'll find some extra sweaters in the front hall

closet if you want to go down to the beach. I
should be back sometime around noon.

Bradley

"Well, Samson, looks like it's just the two of us. What would
you like for breakfast?" Jennifer spoke absently to the dog as
she checked out the contents of the refrigerator and found it to
be well stocked with supplies. Deciding on scrambled eggs and
bacon, she set about cooking something to eat. As the aromas
drifted about the kitchen, Jennifer realized just how hungry she
really was and remembered she had only eaten a light lunch the
day before and no dinner. Samson pushed his empty food dish
across the floor, indicating he, too, was ready for breakfast.

"All right, boy, I get the hint."

A brief search of the cabinets revealed the bag of dog food,
and soon Samson was eagerly gulping down his own canine
gourmet delight.

Jennifer finished preparing her own breakfast and sat
down at the counter. Silently bowing her head, she uttered her
thankfulness to God for His guidance and safe keeping not only
for herself but also for Jarrod.

Eager to explore the magnificent beach that lay just outside
the door, Jennifer quickly finished her meal and washed the few
dishes she had used.

The closet Bradley had mentioned in his note contained a
variety of outerwear, all much too big for Jennifer. After several
tries, she finally located a bulky pullover that at least didn't
swallow her.

Pausing briefly at the top of the staircase to the beach to breathe in the fresh sea air, Jennifer joyfully followed Samson's lead as he bounded easily down the steep wooden planks.

Her laughter at the antics of the dog running ahead of her was lost in the wind, but its healing power was felt deep within the soul of the young beachcomber. The seagulls sang a melody of nature's songs as Jennifer and Samson ran past them on the hard sand of the beach.

Exhausted but happy, Jennifer slowed her pace to a walk as Samson played tag with the incoming waves, more often than not losing to the onrushing water.

A long piece of driftwood deposited halfway between the surf and clumps of sand grass offered the perfect place to rest before Jennifer started the long walk back to the house. Sinking into the warmed sand, Jennifer rested her back against the well-worn log and enjoyed the ever-changing scene before her. Samson too soon tired of his games and joined his new friend in peaceful enjoyment of their surroundings.

The minutes turned into hours as the two lone occupants of the beach savored each minute fluctuation of wave and wind in the space around them.

Suddenly Samson's ears perked up as he listened intently to something new around him. Abruptly he sprang to his feet, began barking, and took off at a run in the direction of the house.

"Samson! What's the matter, boy?" Jennifer called after the rapidly retreating dog as an object no bigger than a dot appeared to be making its way down the beach toward them.

Jennifer watched as the object moved ever closer. Samson cheerfully greeted the intruder by leaping in the air and running circles around the person, still slowly making his way toward the young woman. With a wave of his arm, the stranger sent Samson racing back toward the house.

From Samson's response to the intruder, Jennifer knew he must be a friend. Slowly she too began the trek back to the house.

Each step brought her closer to the person coming slowly, haltingly toward her. A brisk wind suddenly caught his jacket and sent it flying off one shoulder to reveal a large white object covering his arm and shoulder. More often now he paused to rest before continuing his journey.

Suddenly Jennifer stopped. The head of coal black hair and that large frame could only belong to one man.

"Jarrod!" Her heart beat wildly against her breast as she ran as fast as her feet would carry her down the beach, stopping suddenly a few feet away from her visitor.

"What are you doing here?" she asked breathlessly, not sure what to expect as an answer.

"I came looking for you."

"Why?"

"Mainly because I have something to give you." Jarrod slowly withdrew a small package from his pocket and placed it gently in her hand.

"What's this?" Jennifer stared at the tiny silver box tied with a bright blue ribbon, and a card almost as small as the package was tucked securely under the bow.

"It might help if you read the note and then opened it." Jarrod's expression was somber, and Jennifer failed to catch the mischievous glints that sparkled deep in ebony eyes.

Her hand trembling as she pulled at the bow, Jennifer dared not hope that her deepest desires were about to come true.

When she opened the tiny card, tears fill her eyes as she read what Jarrod had written:

> My Darling Jennifer,
>> Someone loves you.
>> Someone cares.
>> Someone whispers your name in prayers.
>> Someone esteems you very high.
>> Yes, God loves you,
>> And so do I.
>> Will you marry me?
>
>>>> Jarrod

"Oh, Jarrod, you know I will." Rushing into his arms, she almost sent them both sprawling onto the sand.

"Darling, I was so afraid I'd lost you again," Jarrod whispered into her hair.

"What do you mean *again*?" Jennifer questioned as she pulled back to study his face.

"Do you remember when you nearly hit me on the highway?" Jennifer blushed at the remembrance. "Well, I'd been praying for God to send me someone to share my life and had just about given up hope. You looked so beautiful and so much in need of comfort that it was all I could do to keep from taking you in my arms right then." Jarrod tenderly brushed the stray tendrils of hair from her face.

"But David said you were such a bear after the accident."

"I was! I knew you were everything I'd ever dreamed of and you were gone. I was so taken back I hadn't even asked your name, where you lived, nothing! It was like a dream—I didn't even know if you were real or I'd just imagined you. Then you walked into my office that morning and I still wasn't sure it was you until your hat fell off and I saw your hair."

"But why didn't you ever let me know?"

"Because the more I learned about you, the more I realized you had some major issues to get straightened out with God before you would be able to enter into the type of meaningful relationship God wants a husband and wife to have."

"And I thought all you were interested in was saving my soul."

"I'll admit I was a little afraid that's all God had intended too. Jennifer, please forgive me for ordering you off the yard. I was heavily sedated and didn't realize what I was saying. I wasn't trusting God to take care of you—like I know He can."

Jennifer reached up and gently caressed the face so close to her own and felt beads of perspiration forming along the creases of his forehead. "Are you all right?"

"I'll be fine," Jarrod assured her as he stopped momentarily to lean against a pile of driftwood.

"How did you get here anyway?"

A boyish grin beamed across his whitening face. "Bradley came down and picked me up at the hospital."

"So that was his important business out of town." Jennifer smiled with pleasure. "We'd better get you back to the house, mister."

"Anything you say, Sarge," he said, giving her a mocking salute.

"Edwards! Edwards was Glen's partner!" Jennifer had almost forgotten about the previous night. "They started the fire and tried to steal the lumber."

"I know."

"You know! But how?"

"Seems Glen has been doing a little talking from his cell after he realized Edwards was going to let him take the fall for everything."

"I don't understand how they could dispose of so much lumber without someone noticing."

"Lumber trucks go up and down Highway 101 all the time and no one pays any attention, but it would take someone who had connections in the business to dispose of it. Bradley did a little checking around last night, and it seems the security company is part of a larger company whose major stockholder is the lumber company that's been trying to buy up all the independents in this part of the country. Through the guards' daily reports, they were able to determine input and output of each mill. Plus they made things nasty for those who wouldn't give in to their offers to sell. They usually had one inside man, and the rest of the crew had no idea they were being used."

They were both quiet for a few minutes, each caught up in their own thoughts and feelings.

"Do you know why I wanted you off graveyard shift?" Jarrod suddenly broke their shared silence as he placed a brief kiss against her temple.

"Probably to ruin my social life," Jennifer said as she snuggled more securely into the crook of his arm.

A soft chuckle rose from his throat. "That was only a side benefit; the main reason was so I could get some sleep."

"What?" She stopped suddenly and looked at his face in disbelief.

"Do you realize just how hard it was for me to be up there on the hill all by myself, knowing you were so close, out there in the rain and cold? I wanted you next to me so I'd know you were safe and warm in my arms."

"Jarrod, I'm right where I'm supposed to be." Jennifer wrapped her arms tightly around Jarrod's waist as two sets of footprints made their way in unison down the tranquil stretch of beach.

CPSIA information can be obtained
at www.ICGtesting.com
Printed in the USA
FFOW03n0304211014
8218FF

9 781490 831046